KEEPING SECRETS

Other books by Maggie Dana

Kate and Holly: The Beginning (Timber Ridge Riders)
Keeping Secrets, Timber Ridge Riders (Book 1)
Racing into Trouble, Timber Ridge Riders (Book 2)
Riding for the Stars, Timber Ridge Riders (Book 3)
Wish Upon a Horse, Timber Ridge Riders (Book 4)
Chasing Dreams, Timber Ridge Riders (Book 5)
Almost Perfect, Timber Ridge Riders (Book 6)
Taking Chances, Timber Ridge Riders (Book 7)
After the Storm, Timber Ridge Riders (Book 8)
Double Feature, Timber Ridge Riders (Book 9)
Flying Changes, Timber Ridge Riders (Book 10)
Horse Camp, Timber Ridge Riders (Book 11)
Something Royal, Timber Ridge Riders (Book 12)
High Stakes, Timber Ridge Riders (Book 13)

Turning on a Dime ~ a time travel adventure
The Golden Horse of Willow Farm, Weekly Reader Books
Remember the Moonlight, Weekly Reader Books
Best Friends series, Troll Books/Scholastic

Sign up for our mailing list and be among the first to know when
the next Timber Ridge Riders book will be out.
Send your email address to:
timberridgeriders@gmail.com

For more information about the series, visit:
www.timberridgeriders.com
Note: all email addresses are kept strictly confidential.

TIMBER RIDGE RIDERS
Book One

KEEPING SECRETS

Maggie Dana

PAGEWORKS PRESS

For Sophie

1

KATE MCGREGOR SKIDDED her aunt's old bike to a stop and stared at the house — gray shingles, white shutters, and a ramp instead of steps. This had to be the right place. Kate pulled the ad from her pocket.

Mature high-school student needed as summer companion for disabled teen. Prefer someone who can live in. Call Timber Ridge Stables at . . .

Beyond the house lay a sprawl of barns, paddocks, and riding rings. In the largest ring, three girls on horseback circled an instructor while another girl jumped a set of parallel bars. Kate stared at them and shook her head. Was she totally nuts? The last thing she needed was a job next door to a horse barn.

Kate dumped her bike on the lawn and ran up the ramp. She knocked on the front door. No answer. She knocked again. The house was quiet . . . too quiet. Had she got the wrong time? The wrong day? She tried the door, but it was locked. She turned to leave and heard somebody yell.

"Help!"

Kate froze.

"Help me out of the water, *please!*"

Sounds of splashing came from somewhere out back. Kate raced around the side of the house, slap bang into a solid stockade fence. No sign of a gate.

"I need help!" More splashing. "Now!"

Grabbing a fence post with both hands, Kate hauled herself up. Her foot slipped, and she landed in the dirt. Now what? She hunted around for something to stand on and found a rusty wheelbarrow lying beneath a bush. That would do. Kate leaned it against the fence, climbed on top, and peered into the backyard.

A girl with hair the color of straw was treading water in a kidney-shaped pool. She raised an arm and cried, "Help me out. *Please!*"

"You don't need any help," another girl said.

Kate turned toward her. The girl was riding a

sweat-covered bay in tight circles just beyond the back fence. The horse tossed its head and pulled at the bit.

"Don't be such a pain," the girl in the pool yelled. "Help me out."

"No way," the other girl said. "I'm not falling for that trick again."

"No tricks. Not this time. I promise."

"Forget it. Last time I helped, you pulled me into the pool." The girl yanked her horse's reins, dug her heels into its sides, and galloped off.

Kate tore her eyes away from the horse and stared at the swimmer. She looked competent and strong. So why did she need help?

Kate's foot slipped again.

Crash!

"Garummmmph!" Kate yelled as she fell off the wheelbarrow.

"Who's there?" It was the girl in the pool.

"Kate McGregor," Kate said through clenched teeth. She brushed the dirt off her legs and stood up. "I'm here about the job."

"Where are you?"

"Behind the fence."

"Can you climb it and help me out?"

"I'll try," replied Kate.

"Hurry." Her voice sounded desperate.

This time the wheelbarrow held. Kate scrambled over the fence and dropped into the backyard. The girl waved at her. Kate frowned. Why would someone who swam like a fish need help getting out of a pool? It didn't make sense.

Then she spotted the wheelchair.

Of course! How could she have been so dumb?

The pool didn't have steps, just a metal ladder. No wonder the girl couldn't get out. Kate dropped to her knees, grasped the girl's arms, and hauled her out of the water.

"Thanks," the girl said, breathing hard. "I was afraid Mom would come back and find me swimming by myself."

Kate pointed at the wheelchair. "Should I help you with this?"

The girl shook her head. "I'll just sit on the edge for a while." She reached for a towel. "I'm Holly Chapman. My mother put the ad in the paper. She needs a watchdog for me."

Kate waved toward the pool. "If you can't get out, how do you get in?"

"Easy," Holly said. "I flop in like a seal. But getting out is always a problem." She looked down at her legs. "They don't work."

"Why wouldn't that girl on the horse help you?"

"Because she's a selfish brat." Holly grinned. "And because she doesn't trust me."

"So you *did* pull her in the pool, then."

"Sure," Holly said. "It was a pool party. Like, duhhh . . . you're supposed to get wet."

"Can she swim?"

Holly bared her teeth. "Like a shark."

"So, what was her problem?"

"New hairdo, new bikini. She didn't want to get them wet."

"So you did it for her?" Kate said. She was starting to like Holly.

"She deserved it. She'd just been mean to one of my friends. Told her she was too fat to wear a bathing suit," Holly said. "And now I bet she's back at the barn telling everyone about my crime."

"Swimming is a crime?"

"Swimming *alone* is a crime," Holly said. "I'd better get dressed. Mom will be here any minute."

"Where is she?"

"At the barn." Holly paused. "But she knows you're coming."

Kate helped Holly into her wheelchair and watched as the girl wheeled herself up the ramp and through the kitchen door.

"Promise not to leave before I get back," Holly yelled before disappearing inside.

"I promise." Kate sat in the shade and waited for Mrs. Chapman to show up.

* * *

"You must be Kate McGregor."

Kate looked up to find a tall, fair-haired woman dressed in riding boots and breeches walking toward her.

"I'm Liz Chapman, Holly's mother," she said, smiling and holding out her hand. "Sorry I wasn't here when you arrived."

"That's okay."

"I had a few problems at the barn."

Kate nodded. She knew all about those.

Liz waved toward the pool. "I'm just glad you were here to pull Holly out before she turned into a prune."

Kate bit back a smile. That girl on the sweaty bay gelding hadn't wasted much time spilling the beans.

"As you've probably gathered, my daughter's a bit headstrong," Liz said. "She needs someone to keep her out of trouble." She paused. "How old are you?"

Kate hesitated. "Almost fifteen." A slight exaggeration. She'd turned fourteen three months ago.

"Have you ever done anything like this before?"

"Like babysitting?"

Liz nodded. "Or looking after elderly people?"

"Holly's not elderly."

"No, but she's just as much work," Liz said. "She's stuck in a wheelchair, she hates people doing things for her, and she takes chances when nobody's looking."

Kate didn't know what to say. She'd never had any kind of a job before that didn't involve horses . . . or her father. "I took care of Dad after my mother died."

"Oh, I'm sorry," Liz said.

"It was a long time ago," Kate said. "My father's useless around the house."

"So am I," Liz said. "Can you cook?"

Kate shrugged. "Macaroni and cheese, fish sticks, peanut-butter-and-jelly sandwiches."

"Fair enough," Liz said. "Do you swim?"

"Yes."

"Good, because swimming's the best exercise for Holly's legs," Liz said. "It helps keep her muscles in shape." She looked at Kate. "You're younger than I'd hoped for, but right now I'm thinking it might be good for Holly to have someone her own age."

Kate crossed her fingers. Hanging out with Holly would be far better than hanging out with Aunt Marion, whose spare bed had more lumps than a bag full of apples.

"If your father agrees, I'd like you to move in with us for the summer," Liz went on. "It'd be easier that way, especially when I have to leave early for horse shows with my students."

"My father's chasing butterflies in Brazil," Kate said. "I'm spending the summer with my aunt."

"How will she feel about you having a job?"

"She'll be glad I've found something to do," Kate said. "I've been driving her crazy. She's not used to kids."

"What about your father?"

"He's not used to them either."

Liz raised an eyebrow. "You're joking."

"No, I'm not," Kate said. "My father's a lepidopterist. If it's got wings, compound eyes, and fuzzy legs, he's all over it. He hasn't got a clue about people."

"But would he mind if you moved in here?"

"I'll ask him tonight."

"How will you reach him?"

"Jungle drums."

Liz laughed.

"Okay, cell phone," Kate said. "That is, if he remembered to turn it on."

"Doesn't he have e-mail?"

"My father?" Kate said. "On the Internet? He's only just figured out how to use a toaster."

"Well, if it's okay with your aunt," Liz said, smiling, "*and* your father, I'll need you till school starts in September."

Kate wanted to know why Holly was in a wheelchair but didn't know how to ask. "Does Holly . . . I mean, has she always been —?"

"Two years ago, Holly was in a car accident," Liz said. "Her father was driving and" — she took a deep breath — "he was killed. Holly hasn't been able to walk since."

"Will she get better?"

"No one really knows," Liz said. "The doctors say there's no permanent damage, but they don't know why she can't use her legs. It might be psychological — something in Holly's mind that prevents her from walking. It's called hysterical paralysis. We've tried numerous treatments; but, so far, nothing's worked."

Wearing a pink t-shirt with *Barn Bum* in big letters across the front, Holly wheeled herself into the backyard. "So, Mom, did you hire her yet?"

"I'm not sure." Liz looked at Kate. "Well?"

Kate hesitated. Did the job include horses? So far, they hadn't been mentioned.

"Kate, please say yes," Holly said. "The last person Mom interviewed had tattoos and bad breath."

"Holly!"

"Well, she did. *And* a nose ring."

A smile flickered across Liz's face. "So, Kate, what do you think?"

"Mrs. Chapman, I —"

"Please, call me Liz."

"Okay," Kate said, not sure she'd be able to do that. She'd never called a grownup by her first name before, not even Mrs. Mueller, her former riding instructor. Kate's mind screeched to a halt. She could hear all the old accusations and felt herself turn pale.

"Kate?"

"Would I have to" — Kate gulped — "go to the barn?"

"I'm glad you brought that up," Liz said.

Oh, no! Kate's heart sank.

10

"I can't afford more than fifty dollars a week; but to make up for lack of money, I'll teach you to ride."

Kate flinched.

"I know it's not much," Liz went on, "but most girls your age love horses and I figured you'd jump at the chance of lessons."

"The money's fine," Kate said. "But I'll pass on the lessons."

"Don't you like horses?" Holly asked.

"No." Kate felt herself going red.

"But *everyone* likes horses."

"I'm sorry," Kate mumbled.

"No need to apologize," Liz said, putting a hand on Kate's arm. "And pay no attention to Holly. Her entire world revolves around horses."

Kate looked away. Before Black Magic died, *her* world had revolved around horses as well. People said it was an accident — a fluke — but Kate blamed herself. Because she hadn't double-checked that stall door, a brilliant show jumper was dead. She shuddered.

"Kate, are you all right?"

"I'm fine." Kate bit her lip. "I'm just scared of horses, that's all," she said, hoping her lie was convincing enough to fool Holly and her mother.

2

"I HOPE YOU DON'T MIND sharing with Holly," Liz said two days later when Kate arrived to begin her new job. "I'm afraid our spare bedroom's full of junk."

"No problem." Kate hefted her suitcase inside.

"Can you manage by yourself?"

"Sure."

"Good, because I'm running late." Liz checked her watch. "I've got lessons all afternoon, but call the barn if you need me. Holly has the number."

"Where should I go?"

"Oh, down there." Liz pointed toward a hall that led off the living room. "See you later."

The door to Holly's room was open. Kate stepped inside. "Hi, I'm —" The words died in her throat.

Holly's room was floor-to-ceiling horses. Posters of

show jumpers and dressage horses covered the walls, and photos of Holly on horseback filled the corkboard above her desk. Ribbons, mostly blue, framed her mirror; red and yellow ribbons hung like bunting around the window. Stuffed ponies snoozed on her bed. A horse mobile dangled above it.

Kate swallowed hard. She'd expected Holly to have some horsey stuff, but this was over the top. *Way* over the top. She dropped her suitcase on the floor beside a wooden rocking horse and scanned the room — shelves crammed with trophies and horse books, a pair of suede chaps dangling from a hook on the door, and pony-print sheets with matching comforter and pillows.

"Holy ravioli!"

"Too much, huh?" Holly said, raising one eyebrow in a perfect imitation of her mother.

Kate shoved a pile of *Young Rider* magazines off a chair and sat down. Sharing Holly's room would be a challenge.

"Mom wants to redecorate," Holly went on, "but I won't let her."

Kate glanced at one of the posters — a Lipizzaner performing a levade — and thought about her bedroom back home, stripped bare of everything that reminded her of horses and Black Magic. How did Holly stand it? Why did she torture herself with memories of something she could no longer do?

"But doesn't this — I mean, how can you bear to, um —?" Kate groped for the right words. "Don't you miss it?"

"Of course, I do."

"So why keep all this?" Kate asked, pointing to a stable full of Breyer models on the dresser. A riding ring and tiny jumps lay beside it.

"Incentive."

Kate stared at her. "Huh?"

"It forces me to keep hoping." Holly's mouth hardened. "Sometimes it makes me angry." She sucked in her breath. "But mostly it reminds me that, one day, I'm going to ride again."

"Are you sure? I mean, didn't the doctors —?"

"Yeah, yeah, I know what they said, and none of them can agree. But *I* think it's all in my head. It *has* to be. My spine is okay. There's no nerve damage, no brain damage" — Holly grimaced and slapped her forehead — "well, not much, anyway."

She handed Kate the *Equus* magazine she'd been holding in her lap. "Look at this. I might be riding sooner than you think."

Skimming the page, Kate saw a photo of a boy in leg braces riding a fat brown pony. The caption beneath it said:

Ten-year-old Tim Sullivan can ride his pony even though he can't walk, thanks to the volunteers at the Vermont Therapeutic Riding Association.

"If Tiny Tim can do it," Holly said, her blue eyes flashing with determination, "so can I."

Kate hesitated. "Does your Mom know about this?"

"Not yet, but let's go and tell her."

"Now?"

"Why not?" Holly wheeled herself to the door.

"Because she's busy with riding lessons," Kate said. "And I'd like to unpack."

"You can do that later."

Kate felt herself tense up. She'd been on the job less than half an hour, and already Holly wanted to visit the barn. "I'm really hot. Let's go jump in the pool."

"Okay," Holly said. "Pool first, barn later." She paused. "How fast can you swim?"

Kate shrugged. "I was on the swim team last year."

"Then let's race."

"Are you sure?" Kate said.

15

"Why not?"

"Well, your legs. I mean —"

"Come on." Holly pulled two towels from a pile on the floor. She grinned and tossed one to Kate. "Eat my wake."

* * *

Kate tried, but no matter which stroke she used, Holly beat her. Exhausted and out of breath, Kate admitted defeat and left Holly in the pool, swimming laps to exercise her legs.

Kate wrapped herself in a towel, lay down on a chaise, and worried about the barn. What excuse, besides fear, could she give for not going? *Allergies? Hey, that might work.* She sat up, held her nose, and faked a sneeze.

"Arrrggghhh-schnoorrr!"

"You okay?" Holly yelled.

Kate sniffed. "Hay fever."

"Could've fooled me." Holly swam to the ladder. "I thought we'd been invaded by donkeys."

Kate pulled Holly out of the pool. "This ladder's a pain."

"Tell me about it."

"Couldn't your mom put in real steps?"

"Too expensive," Holly said, shaking out her hair and spraying Kate with drops of water. "Besides, the pool isn't ours."

"Oh, but I thought —"

Holly swept her arm through the air. "This pool, the house, everything. It's all part of Mom's job."

"So who owns it, then?"

"The almighty Timber Ridge Homeowners' Association," Holly said. "They also own the golf course, the tennis courts, the swimming pool, the ski area, *and* the stables."

Shielding her eyes from the sun, Kate looked up at Timber Ridge Mountain. Grass-covered ski trails spilled from its peak like dribbles of green paint. Without thinking, she said, "Do you ski?"

Holly made a choking sound.

"I can't believe I said that," Kate said. "I'm sorry. I'm really, really sorry."

"It's okay," Holly replied. "And, no, I never skied. I've got two left feet."

"So do I," Kate said, "and right now, they're both in my mouth."

Holly grinned. She wheeled herself up the ramp and into the kitchen. She opened the fridge, pulled out two apples, and gave one to Kate. "Look, I know you don't like horses, and that's okay. You don't have to come to the barn. I can handle it by myself."

Kate shook her head. Liz was paying her to do a job, and no way would she let her down. "I'll come," she said. "I'll just bring lots of tissues and stay outside."

"Don't you have allergy medicine?"

"Um, no. I mean, yes," Kate said, thinking fast. "But I left it at my aunt's."

"Will you be okay?"

"Sure." Kate ran a hand through her shoulder-length brown hair and tied it back with an elastic. It still felt weird, not having a braid that reached to her waist. She'd cut it off the day after Black Magic died. Her father hadn't noticed for a week.

Holly said, "If we hurry, you'll get to see Mom's team in action."

"Team?"

"Riding team."

Kate took a bite of apple and followed Holly down the hall and into her room. *Their* room, now. The sight of all those horses set her teeth on edge. Holly was cool, but her bedroom was the pits. No way could Kate live in it for the next two months. Maybe Liz would let her clean out the spare room. But how could she pull it off without hurting Holly's feelings? She'd have to come up with another dumb excuse, like Holly snored or talked in her sleep. Sheesh! This lying business was getting way too complicated.

"They're getting ready for the Hampshire County Classic. It's the biggest show of the season," Holly said, reaching into a drawer for a t-shirt. "Mom's really sweating it."

"Why?"

"If the team doesn't win blue ribbons, Mom's contract to run the stables won't be renewed" — Holly pulled the t-shirt over her head — "which means Mom would have to find another job and somewhere else for us to live."

"That's awful!"

"I know. It stinks." Holly leaned down to tie her sneakers. "Everything was fine till Angela Dean's mother got involved."

"Who's Angela?"

"The brat who wouldn't help me out of the pool."

Kate grinned. "Swims like a shark?"

Holly nodded. "Before Mrs. Dean interfered, Mom ran the stables the way *she* wanted. The kids had fun, they learned to ride and take care of their horses, and nobody cared if they won or lost."

"Is Angela's mom *that* bad?"

"Trust me." Holly stuck a finger in her mouth and pretended to gag. "She makes Lady Macbeth look like Malibu Barbie."

Kate grinned. "You're exaggerating."

"Just wait till you meet her," Holly warned. "You'll see what I mean. She's the worst kind of horse-show mother. If Angela doesn't win, Mrs. Dean has a fit and takes it out on Angela, then blames Mom, which is totally unfair."

"How does Angela feel about this?"

"What do you think?"

"Makes life miserable for the rest of you?"

"You're catching on fast," Holly said.

Kate shuddered. She'd met mothers like Mrs. Dean before. Every stable had them.

"Come on," Holly said. "Let's go find Mom. I can't wait to show her this." She picked up the magazine. "You really don't have to come."

"I'll be okay."

Holly crammed a faded pink baseball hat on her head. It had *Boss Mare* embroidered in black above the peak. "Don't worry about the horses. They're not running wild all over the place. We keep them penned up most of the time."

Kate forced a smile, but her stomach was doing backflips, and she could feel the sweat on her hands where they gripped the handles of Holly's wheelchair.

"I'm okay," she whispered to herself. "I'm okay."

Who was she kidding?

* * *

Angela Dean turned her horse toward the barn and glanced at her mother, leaning against her silver Mercedes on the other side of the fence. If only she didn't insist on watching every lesson. None of the other mothers did.

"Okay, Angela," Liz yelled from the center of the ring. "Try the double oxer again, and this time, don't keep such a tight rein. Relax. Let Skywalker have his head. He knows what he's doing."

Angela cringed. Her mother would give her the third degree about this later. She always did. Angela clamped her legs against Skywalker's belly and twisted her fingers through his mane. The jump was almost four feet. It looked enormous.

"Don't you dare refuse!" Angela muttered as her horse cantered toward it. He'd already run out twice, and she was determined to get him over it . . . one way or another. With Mother watching, she didn't have much choice.

* * *

"Who's that?" Kate asked, knowing full well it was Angela Dean. She recognized the horse.

"Princess Angela," Holly said.

Horse and rider approached the jump.

"Is she a good rider?" Kate asked, playing dumb.

"Not really."

"She looks okay to me," Kate said, cringing inwardly as Angela jerked the bay's mouth. He put in an extra stride, took off too late, and rapped the top bar with his forelegs. It wobbled but didn't fall.

"That's because Skywalker's a push-button horse," Holly replied. "Push the right ones and he performs."

"What happens if he doesn't?"

"Mrs. Dean would sell him for dog food."

"You're kidding."

"She sent their last horse to auction because Angela couldn't control him." Holly spat out the words. "I can only imagine where he ended up."

Skywalker's hooves kicked up clouds of dust as he pounded down the track. His nostrils flared. His sides heaved. Sweat had turned his mahogany coat into a froth of swirls. As he flashed by, Kate looked up and caught a glimpse of Angela's face, pinched with anger.

"I'm surprised she's even riding," Holly said. "Angela hates lessons. Says she doesn't need to practice."

Just then, Liz noticed them and waved before turning to a girl on a dappled gray mare. "Robin, you're next."

The girl aimed her horse at the jump. Their approach was crooked, and Kate thought they were going to refuse. But Robin urged the mare forward. She responded and popped over it like a cat.

"Much better than last time," Liz called out. "I like the way you kept Chantilly going."

She beckoned to the last horse and rider. "This one shouldn't give you any trouble, Susan. Go ahead."

"That's my horse, Magician," Holly said, as the big black gelding thundered toward the green-and-white oxer. "Isn't he gorgeous?" She grabbed Kate's arm. "I know it's stupid, but I can almost feel my legs wrapped around him."

But Kate wasn't listening. She let out a gasp. It couldn't be, could it? Her eyes were playing tricks . . . they had to be.

3

KATE RUBBED THE DUST from her eyes and peered at Holly's horse between her fingers. This was beyond scary. Magician looked exactly like Black Magic: a deep, dark brown — so dark, he was almost black, with not a speck of white anywhere. Magician had the same proud head with small ears pricked forward; the same arched neck and well-muscled shoulders; and the same strong, compact body that ended in powerful hindquarters and a long, flowing tail. Kate trembled and felt the same excitement she'd always felt when watching Black Magic jump.

Except it wasn't him. Magic was dead, and she'd killed him. Kate held onto the rail and tried to stop shaking.

Magician cleared the jump with two feet to spare.

"Perfect," Liz called out to his rider. "Okay, that's enough for today."

She walked across the ring toward Holly and Kate but stopped when she saw Angela sitting on Skywalker down by the gate. "Angela, why aren't you cooling him off?"

Angela shrugged. "He's fine."

"No, he's not," Liz said, sounding grim. "He's sweating. If you don't walk him out, he'll colic. Go and join the others. They're in the back paddock taking care of their horses."

"Whatever," Angela said, picking up her reins. "Anything else?"

"Go," Liz said. "Just go." Her shoulders slumped. Her face looked drained and tired, and Kate felt sorry for her.

"Poor Mom," Holly said.

"Is Angela always like this?"

Holly scowled. "She's usually much worse."

"Does your mom *have* to teach her?"

"She doesn't have a choice," Holly said. "Remember? Mrs. Dean runs everything around here."

Liz ducked under the fence.

"Mom," Holly said, thrusting the magazine toward her. "You've got to read this. It's about disabled kids who're riding."

"I know," Liz said. "I've read it."

"What?" Holly exploded. "And you didn't tell me?"

Liz shook her head.

"Why not?" demanded Holly.

"Because you'd hate it."

"Wrong!" Holly said. "I'd love it."

Liz held up her hands. "Stop and think for a minute. Most of those kids have never ridden before. They're doing this for therapy, to help their bodies move and function."

"So?" Holly said. "Don't I need that as well?"

"Yes," Liz said, "but you've ridden all your life. You know what it feels like. You were good. *Really* good. And this won't be the same. You'll get frustrated. You'll hate it, and —"

"No, I won't!" Holly said, shaking her head so hard her ponytail whipped back and forth. "I'd give anything to ride Magician again."

"Whoa, Holly. Stop right there." Liz put a hand on Holly's shoulder. "Your horse needs a strong pair of legs around him. You ought to know that."

Holly stuck out her lower lip. "Then I'll ride Plug."

"Who's Plug?" Kate asked.

"My first pony," Holly said. "Mom uses him for beginner lessons."

Liz sighed. "Oh, Holly. I just don't know. You riding Plug would be like an Olympic skier going down the . . . um . . . the —"

"Bunny slope?" Kate offered.

"Exactly." Liz shot her quick look of thanks.

"I don't care," Holly said. "I'll ride anything."

"Even Plug?"

Holly nodded vigorously. "He's sweet and gentle, and he's quiet as a mouse."

"And stubborn as a stone," said Liz.

"Please, Mom."

"Okay. You win." Liz sighed. "But I can't do it without help."

"So call them," Holly said. "Their phone number's in the article."

"Are you sure about this?"

"Positive," said Holly.

"Then I'll ask one of their volunteers to come and help me get started." Liz turned toward Kate. "But I'll need someone else as well."

Hating herself, Kate said, "I'm sorry, but I —"

"Kate doesn't like horses, remember?" Holly said. "And she's allergic to hay." She paused. "Couldn't one of the other kids help out?"

"Yes, but I still need someone to get you over here."

"Mom," Holly protested. "I can do it myself."

Liz shook her head. "The path between here and the house is full of ruts. If you hit one and fall out of your chair, then —"

"So I'll use the road," Holly said.

"It's too far and besides, it's uphill."

Kate cleared her throat. "I'll do it. I'll bring Holly to the barn."

"Thanks." Liz smiled at her.

Holly grabbed Kate's hand. "Come see Magician with me."

Kate pulled away. She scrunched up her nose and fumbled for a tissue. It was time for another sneeze.

"Don't push her," Liz warned.

"Kate, please," Holly said. "Just for a few minutes. *Please*. You don't have to stay long if you don't want to."

It was tempting. Oh, so tempting. The smells, the sounds of horses pacing their stalls waiting for food. Kate could feel herself racing to the feed room and scooping grain into buckets, staggering down the aisle beneath armloads of hay so fresh you wanted to bury your face in it. She tried to step back, but guilt had bolted her feet to the ground.

"Come on," Holly said. "Let's go."

Kate looked at the barn with its weathervane and cupola and faded red siding. The double doors were open, beckoning her inside.

The other kids were in there, brushing sweat from their horses and settling them in for the night. Kate could hear them laughing and talking about their lesson and their chances in the upcoming competition. Was it only three months ago that she'd done the same things? It seemed like a lifetime.

"Okay, let's go." Kate gripped Holly's chair and pushed. *Don't think. Just do it. Pretend that knot of guilt in your stomach is that pizza you ate for lunch.*

Kate steered Holly's wheelchair toward the barn. Holly kept on talking, about how Sue Piretti was the only one good enough to ride Magician and about how fabulous it was that Robin Shapiro had done so well with Chantilly. This was her first year on the team.

They plunged into the barn's cool, dim interior. Two cats skittered across the aisle. Barn swallows chirped in the rafters. A horse whinnied. So did another. Kate tightened her grip on Holly's chair. *It's okay, you can do it. One foot in front of the other.* Feed room on the right. Tack room on the left. Liz's office just beyond it. Hayloft above. Twelve stalls, six on each side. Rakes, pitchforks, and brooms leaning against walls. Red plastic muck buckets with rope handles, full of manure. Tack trunks. A hoof pick lying in the sawdust. Someone's curry comb spilled from a grooming box. The smell of fresh hay.

Kate breathed it all in and hated herself all over again.

"Magician!" Holly reached up to unlatch a stall door. It slid open. She wheeled herself inside.

Kate stared at the latch. If only she'd checked. If only she'd gone back and made sure that miserable door was locked. If she had, Black Magic would still be alive.

Inside the stall, Holly said, "Sue, he looked fabulous out there."

"You think so?" said another voice. It belonged to a girl with freckles and short, sandy hair. She was brushing Magician with strong, methodical strokes. His coat gleamed like coal.

"Are you ready for the Hampshire?" Holly said.

Sue grinned. "We'd better be. Your mom's been drilling us for weeks."

"This time, you'll win, for sure," Holly said. "You came so close last year."

Sue brandished her brush. "I'm practicing my stable management."

Their voices dropped and Kate caught the names "Angela" and "Denise." Her nose twitched. Her eyes filled and she sneezed . . . for real, this time.

"Hey, Sue, this is Kate," Holly said. "Kate, meet Sue Piretti."

"Come and join the party," Sue said. "Magician won't mind."

Kate stood her ground. "No, thanks."

"Um, Sue," Holly said, "Kate's not too fond of horses. She's better off out there."

"Oh, sure." Sue went back to brushing Holly's horse.

Magician dropped his nose and nibbled gently at Holly's hand. She fed him a carrot. He nuzzled her face, then rested his great black head in her lap.

"You big silly," she said, wrapping her arms around him. She fondled his ears and laid her cheek against his. Magician whickered.

Gulping back tears, Kate looked away. Her eyelids

pricked. A huge lump blocked her throat. Behind her, someone said, "So, Holly, aren't you going to introduce me to your new slave?"

Kate turned and found herself face-to-face with pale blue eyes and masses of dark hair. It was hot and sticky, yet Angela Dean looked as if she'd just stepped from an advertisement for Devon-Aire riding clothes. Her yellow shirt was spotless, her boots shone, and her buff breeches didn't look as if she'd just spent a grueling hour in the saddle.

"Aren't you supposed to be brushing Skywalker?" Holly said, wheeling herself out of Magician's stall.

Angela shrugged. "Denise is doing it for me."

"That's *your* job," Holly said.

Magician pushed past her chair and into the aisle.

"Get back, you silly horse!" Holly grabbed his halter.

Kate jumped and fell against the wall, feigning fear.

"What's the matter?" Angela sneered at Kate. "Scared of a big pussycat like Magician?"

"Leave her alone," Holly snapped.

Sue led Magician back into his stall.

"Angela, why is Denise brushing your horse?" Liz strode up holding a bridle. "I found this outside Skywalker's stall. I believe it's yours." She thrust it toward Angela.

"Ugh, it's got manure all over it."

"What do you expect?" Liz glared at her. "It was flung on the ground. I suggest you clean it immediately . . . *after* you take care of your horse."

"I don't have time. Mother's waiting for me," Angela said. "We have guests coming for dinner." She flicked her hair away from her face and walked off.

Wiping her hands on a cloth, Sue stepped out of Magician's stall. "My mother would kill me if I acted like that."

"Bratface," Holly muttered.

If Liz heard, she gave no sign. "Susan, please take this to the tack room for me." She handed her the bridle. "And don't you dare clean it. Angela can ride with dirty tack tomorrow. Maybe she'll learn something."

While Sue took off with Angela's bridle, Holly went back inside Magician's stall. Liz disappeared into her office, and Kate was left on her own.

She looked at Magician. Holly was feeding him the last of her carrots. It was uncanny how his ears flopped to half-mast the way Black Magic's had done. Memories, unbidden and unwanted, flooded back, like the time last winter when she brought Magic and the other horses in from the paddock. It was dark and the ground was icy. She slipped and fell. The horses behind Magic pushed. One bit his rump as if to say, *Hurry up — move on.* But Magic stood his ground, protecting her, while she struggled to her feet. He'd kept her from being trampled by the rest of the herd.

Holly wheeled herself out of Magician's stall. "I'm ready for another swim. How about you?"

"You bet." Kate pushed Holly outside, took a deep lungful of fresh air, and shivered with relief. It was over. She'd survived.

"Angela's still here," Holly said.

Kate glanced toward the Mercedes. Angela, hands on her hips, leaned against the hood. Mrs. Dean, tall and thin, towered over her. Their voices carried across the parking lot.

"Of course, I'll be on the team." Angela reached past her mother for the door handle. "I'm the best rider they've got."

"I hope so," Mrs. Dean answered, her voice cool and distant. "I paid a fortune for that horse. Your father and I will be extremely disappointed if you don't win the Hampshire."

"Don't worry," Angela said, shooting a venomous look at Holly and Kate. "I'll win." She climbed in and slammed the car door.

Holly winced. "You're on Angela's hit list now."

"Why?"

"Because you heard Mom telling her off, and now you've just heard this." Holly nodded toward the departing Mercedes. "*And* she knows you're scared of horses. She'll enjoy taunting you about that."

"Then I'll just have to keep out of her way," Kate replied.

"That'll be tough," Holly said. "You'll be bringing me to the barn every day from now on."

So I will, Kate thought. *Let's hope I can handle it.*

4

THAT NIGHT, HOLLY CRUISED THE WEB. She found site after site filled with information about therapeutic riding for disabled kids.

"Look at this," Holly said. "In Europe they're using retired dressage horses to help people like me." She pointed to a picture on the screen. "See that horse? He was in the Beijing Olympics."

Kate crossed her fingers behind her back. "What's dressage?"

"A way of training horses to be supple, balanced, and responsive," Liz said, coming into Holly's room with an armload of laundry, "which makes them more comfortable to ride."

Holly pushed away from her computer. "Mom, did you call yet?"

"One of their volunteers, Pat Randolph, will be here in the morning."

"Cool," Holly said. "Thanks, Mom."

Liz turned to Kate. "Can you bring Holly to the barn tomorrow?"

Kate looked at Holly's face, pink with excitement. How could she refuse? "What time?"

"Eleven o'clock."

"Okay." No way could she rain on Holly's parade. Besides, it was her job. It's what Liz was paying her to do.

* * *

The butterflies in Kate's stomach had turned into bats by the time they reached the barn. She forced herself inside. Liz and the other kids were still in the outside ring, winding up another team practice. There was no sign of the volunteer.

"You don't have to stay," Holly said. She trundled into the tack room and came out with a box of grooming tools on her knee. "Go," she said to Kate. "I know you hate it in here, and you'll probably start sneezing."

Kate ran outside and sat down beneath a tree. In the distance, she heard Liz's team leave the ring, laughing and talking. Only Angela's voice was missing. She tried to read, but her eyes refused to focus. She kept thinking about Holly and what she must be feeling — riding a horse again. Holly had problems . . . *huge* problems. She couldn't walk, yet she was trying to ride. And here was Kate, too chicken to go and watch. Shame surged up her throat. It tasted worse than vomit. Swallowing hard, Kate forced herself to read, but all she did was stare at the same page for ten minutes.

This was ridiculous. How could she be such a wimp?

Easy. She was downright scared — scared of her feelings, scared of being scared. It was *her* fault Black Magic had died. If she'd checked that stupid latch, he wouldn't have gotten out and —

Kate counted to ten and scrambled to her feet. She wasn't a coward. She *would* go and watch.

She slipped into the indoor arena and hid in the shadows. Holly sat erect on the brown pony, legs hanging way below his belly. She looked like a kid on her first pony ride with Liz walking on one side and the volunteer on the other.

Holly's face, lit by a smile, said it all.

I'm riding again.

"I can't believe it," Holly said, over and over. "I'm riding."

"And you're doing great," Pat Randolph said. "Try and feel the rhythm of the pony as he walks. Let your body relax and move with him." She put her hands on Holly's hips. "The three-dimensional movement of the horse closely resembles the movement of the human pelvis while walking. Can you feel it, Holly?"

"Yes," Holly said. "Yes, I can."

Liz smiled and patted her daughter's leg. "Let me walk with her, Pat. Stand back, and tell me if we're doing it right."

They made a small circle around the volunteer.

"Think I'll be ready for next Olympics?" Holly said.

"Not till you can jump the parallel bars with no stirrups," Pat replied.

Holly grinned. "That comes *next* week."

At the end of the lesson, Holly was so excited she couldn't stop talking about it.

"Kate, you've got no idea what it feels like," she said, once Pat Randolph had left. "You *must* take lessons. Just think what fun we could have riding together." She leaned forward and rubbed her hand up and down Plug's wiry mane.

Kate didn't trust herself to answer. She was light-years away from riding a horse again. But being in the barn wasn't quite as painful as it had been the day before. Maybe Holly's example inspired her . . . or else shamed her. She wasn't sure which. She followed Liz and the pony to the stables and felt some of the old excitement coming back.

* * *

Three days later, Kate found herself standing outside Magician's stall. The horse pricked his ears and whickered. He thrust his soft nose between the bars as if hoping for a carrot.

"I think he likes you," Liz said, as she led Plug into his stall. Holly had just finished her second lesson.

"He's beautiful," Kate said, unable to take her eyes off Holly's horse. Now that she knew him better, he didn't remind her so painfully of Black Magic. He'd taken on his own personality, and he'd become a magnet she couldn't resist.

"Are you sure you don't want riding lessons?" Liz asked. She closed the door to Plug's stall.

Kate wanted to shout YES at the top of her voice. Instead, she said, "Thanks, but I'd rather just watch."

* * *

The next afternoon, Angela and her best friend, Denise Elliott, showed up in the middle of Holly's riding lesson. Angela wore pink wristbands that matched her short skirt. She carried an expensive-looking tennis racquet. Denise flicked a lock of auburn hair from her face, then adjusted the white sweater that hung around her shoulders.

"Get a load of the country club set," Holly muttered to Kate as she rode by on Plug. Her lessons were going so well that she no longer needed Liz to help hold her in the saddle. Earlier, she'd announced she was going to trot.

Kate glanced at Angela and moved farther down the rail. As Holly had predicted, Angela never missed an opportunity to make fun of her, and today Kate was in no mood for the girl's spiteful tongue. The day before, she'd handed Kate a green polo shirt with the words *Timber Ridge* embroidered above the pocket. "All the hired help wear these," Angela had said. "And look how well it matches your eyes." Holly had snatched it from Kate's hands and thrown it into a muck bucket.

"Hey, Holly," Angela drawled. "Denise told me

you're hoping to take her place on the team. She's really worried, so we've come to check you out."

Holly's face flushed. She whipped around in the saddle and glared at Angela. "You —"

"Holly, be careful!" Kate yelled.

Too late. Without strong legs to keep her firmly in the saddle, Holly toppled off the pony's back.

For a split second, Kate couldn't move. Holly lay like a rag doll on the ground, arms outstretched, one leg folded beneath the other. Was it broken? Kate raced across the arena.

"Holly, are you okay?" Kate gasped, as Liz ran up to join them.

Holly groaned. "I'm all right." With Kate's help, she sat up and wiped flecks of tanbark off her face.

"You scared me," Kate said.

Liz grasped Holly's hand. "Me, too."

"I *hate* her," Holly said. "Angela did this on purpose. If I could walk, I'd go over there right now and —"

"Leave this to me," Liz said. "I'll speak to her mother."

"Mom, be careful," Holly said. "Mrs. Dean's worse than Angela."

"Stop worrying. I'll take care of it."

Kate glanced toward the fence, but Angela and Denise had vanished. Had they really wanted to make Holly fall off? Were they *that* mean and vicious? And if so, why? Holly wasn't a threat to either of them. She wasn't the star rider any more.

"Are you sure you're all right?" Liz said. "Do you feel dizzy?"

"No, I'm fine," Holly said in a tight voice. "But I've had enough for today. Could someone get my chair?"

"Where is it?" Kate said.

"In the barn."

Plug wandered up to investigate. He lowered his nose and nuzzled Holly's head.

"Take the pony with you," Liz said.

Without thinking, Kate reached for Plug's reins, then realized she was supposed to be scared. She hesitated, not sure what to do next.

"Mom," Holly said, "Kate doesn't like horses, remember?"

Kate shrugged and tried to laugh it off. Liz said it was no problem. She'd take care of the pony if Kate would just get Holly's chair.

There was no sign of Angela or Denise in the barn. Good thing, Kate thought, or she'd have been tempted to punch them. She found Holly's chair outside Magician's stall. He whickered at her again.

"You beautiful horse," Kate whispered. Then she reached for the latch. Could she do it? Her fingers trembled as she slid the bolt to one side. The door opened, and Magician pricked his ears. He took a step toward her. Closer. Kate held her breath. Gently, the horse nuzzled her hands, her pockets.

If only she'd thought to bring a carrot. But how could she have known this would happen? Slowly, she raised her arms and put them around his neck. She buried her face in his mane and breathed in his familiar, horsey smell. As she leaned into him, memories she'd been trying to bury, tumbled through her mind. Black Magic jumping a clear round in the finals. Their almost perfect dressage test. That incredible ride over the cross-country course when they'd beaten the clock and everyone else.

Kate let him go and shrank against the wall. No, this wasn't right. She had no business hugging Holly's horse or anyone else's for that matter.

5

THOUGHTS OF MAGICIAN HAUNTED Kate for the next
three days. She couldn't get him out of her mind. So
when Holly suggested they go and watch Sue and
Robin practice on the cross-country course, Kate
agreed. It was Friday afternoon, and Liz had just driven
off to attend a dressage clinic in New Hampshire. All
their chores were done, and they were free to enjoy the
rest of the day. Armed with water bottles and bug re-
pellent, they headed for the trails at the base of Timber
Ridge Mountain. Holly said the best place to watch
was a grassy knoll in a clearing that overlooked two
jumps and a stream.

"How much farther?" Kate asked. They were deep
into the woods, at least a mile from the barn. Sweat
trickled down her neck. Her shoulders ached. Pushing

Holly's chair up the unpaved road was hard work, even though its fat wheels were specially designed for rough terrain.

"Not far." Holly put a hand to her ear. "Here they come now."

Kate could hear hoofbeats, moving fast. Too fast for the uneven ground. As she looked up, a riderless horse shot into view, stirrups flying, loose reins whipping around its legs.

"*What —?*"

Holly's horse thundered past. Sparks flew from his metal shoes as they struck rocks and gravel.

"*Magician!*" Holly screamed.

Amid a shower of dirt, he skidded to a halt, turned, and lowered his head. "Come here," Holly said, holding out her hand. It was shaking. She looked up at Kate. "Sue must've fallen off. You'll have to find her."

Kate's stomach did flip-flops as Magician sidled up, nostrils distended, eyes focused on Holly. He whickered and stuck his nose in Holly's lap. She grabbed his bridle. "He's wet," she said, running her hands down his face. "They were probably in the stream."

"Which way?" Kate said.

Holly pointed. "About two hundred yards." She

cupped her mouth and yelled. "Sue . . . Robin. Where are you?"

No answer.

"Will you be okay by yourself?" Kate asked.

"Yes, but hurry. Sue might be hurt." Holly reached for her cell phone. "I'll call for help."

Kate raced into the woods. Brambles scratched her bare legs as she followed the path, jumping rocks and running through mud that wanted to suck off her sneakers. She glanced behind, but the undergrowth was so dense, she couldn't see Holly or Magician any more. How far had she gone? A hundred yards? More?

Pushing a low branch out of her way, she stepped into a small clearing and paused to listen. She heard nothing except the sound of running water. No voices. Nobody calling for help.

The stream Holly mentioned glittered through the trees, but there was no sign of a fallen rider. Kate climbed the knoll. Was that a jump or a pile of logs between those two birches? And how about that rock wall? Was this the place Holly had in mind? If so, she had to be dreaming. No way could Kate have gotten Holly this far into the woods. The trail wasn't wide enough for a bike, let alone a wheelchair.

Hoofprints pockmarked the ground, and they looked fresh. So Kate followed them down the slope and back into the woods. Grass gave way to ruts and puddles. Rocks and leaves littered the path.

"Sue?" she called. "Robin?" No answer.

Louder, she hollered, "Sue, where are you?"

A mosquito landed on her arm. Swatting it, Kate ran toward the logs. It *was* a jump, and something lay sprawled across the path behind it.

Blue shirt, black boots, buff breeches smeared with mud.

"Sue," Kate yelled. She clambered over the logs and crouched beside Holly's friend. "Sue, wake up. Are you okay?"

Of course, she isn't okay. She's unconscious.

Half-remembered first-aid instructions shot through Kate's mind. Check for a pulse. Loosen collar. Don't move the victim.

Victim?

Kate gulped and touched Sue's shoulder. She moaned and blinked twice, then opened her eyes. One side of her face looked as if a cat had sharpened its claws on it. Blood oozed from a cut on her lip. Her left eye had the beginnings of a real shiner.

"Where am I?" Sue mumbled.

Kate's breath came out in a rush. "What happened?"

Sue's lips barely moved. "The jump. I . . . we fell."

"Where's Robin?" Kate looked around.

"Gone . . . she went to meet her family." Sue put a hand to her forehead and groaned. "They're camping at the lake."

That was two miles away.

"Think you can get up?" Kate asked.

Sue nodded and tried to stand, but her legs gave out and she collapsed in a heap. "My head hurts," she whispered, pulling off her helmet.

Kate took a quick look, but she didn't see any blood in Sue's hair. No swelling, either. Okay, now what should she do? Stay here with Sue and hope Holly reached someone by cell phone, or run back to the barn for help?

Faintly, she heard Holly's voice, calling her name.

"Don't move," Kate said.

Sue's mouth twitched into a smile. "Not much chance of that."

"I'll get help."

"Where's Magician?" Sue asked. "Is he okay?"

"He's fine," Kate said, scrambling to her feet. "Holly has him."

She retraced her steps at full speed and burst onto the dirt road in such a rush she startled Magician. He jerked his head, and Holly almost let go of him.

"Did you find her?" she said.

"Yes," Kate said. Breathing hard, she doubled over.

"Is she okay?"

"She's conscious and nothing's broken, but she's pretty banged up. Her face looks as if she tangled with a tiger."

"What about Robin?"

Kate straightened and shook her head. "She went to meet her family at the lake, so Sue rode on alone."

Holly groaned. "Mom will kill them for this."

"Did you call for help?"

"No," Holly wailed. "My stupid cell phone doesn't get service out here." She paused. "You'll have to run for the barn. Go, now. Quickly."

Bursting with energy, Magician chomped on his bit. His shoulders gleamed with sweat, his hooves beat a tattoo on the ground. He needed to run. So did Kate, but it would take ten minutes to reach the barn on foot. Maybe fifteen. She stared at Holly's horse, at the empty saddle, waiting for her. Could she do it? Could she stick her foot in that stirrup and haul herself onto his back? She'd be home in five minutes — less if she took a shortcut over the cross-country course. Sue was hurt and she needed help.

Now.

"Kate, hurry up."

Go on. You can do it. You don't have a choice.

Before she had a chance to chicken out, Kate grabbed the pommel and vaulted into Holly's saddle. Magician skittered sideways, snorting and tossing his head.

Holly exploded. "Kate, you can't. Stop. You'll get hurt."

Not daring to look at Holly, Kate gathered up her reins and dug her heels into Magician's sides. He spun in a circle, then leaped forward like a coiled spring. His legs pounded the trail and within seconds, Holly's frantic yells were drowned by the noise of Magician's hooves and Kate's thumping heart.

Stunned by what she'd just done, Kate swallowed hard and forced herself into Magician's rhythm. Was she really on his back? Riding? Were these *her* legs wrapped around a horse, galloping like a wild thing?

Rocks and trees flashed past. Low branches tore at her hair. Where was the trail Holly pointed out that led back to the barn? Had they passed it already? Magician veered to the right. He knew the way home. They plunged down a bank, into the woods.

Kate leaned forward, urging him to move faster. He leaped a ditch and soared over a fallen tree trunk, and each ground-covering strike drew Kate more deeply into him until she felt as if they were joined through the saddle. His legs became her legs. His body was part of hers, like a centaur. It all seemed so natural, so easy. She was on a horse, and she wasn't coming unglued.

Yet.

The important thing was getting help for Sue. She'd deal with her own feelings, her guilt, after all this was over. The woods opened into a field. Jumps lay around its perimeter, but none stood between her and the barn except for the back gate. Kate prayed it was open, otherwise she'd have to stop and get off. More time wasted.

The gate was closed.

It wasn't that high, a shade under four feet. Magician tossed his head and danced sideways, jiggling his bit. Flecks of foam flew from his mouth and stuck to his shoulders like miniature marshmallows.

What are you waiting for? he seemed to be saying.
Come on. Let's go.

Kate gripped the saddle and winced as the stirrup
leathers bit into her bare knees. Fingers cramped with
tension, she clutched Magician's mane for dear life.
This was a really dumb move. *Stop now, before it's too
late. Get off and open the gate.* But Magician had other
ideas. With a flick of his ears, he shot forward. She
couldn't stop him.

Then, they were airborne, floating, weightless.

Wonderful.

Whump!

They landed, safe on the other side.

Had anyone seen them? Kate waited for angry cries,
but none came. The barn felt eerily deserted. She trotted through the indoor arena and into the stables.
Nobody there. What a relief. Kate slid off Magician's
back. Her legs folded like silly putty.

"Don't move," she warned, reaching for the wall
phone outside Liz's office. She punched in 911 and
panted out the details of where to find Sue and Holly.
Then she rang Mrs. Piretti, who said she'd be right
there and asked if she should stop to pick up Kate, too.

Kate glanced at Magician, sides heaving, steam
rising from his sweat-covered rump and shoulders. "I'd

better stay here," she told Mrs. Piretti. No way could she leave Holly's horse in this state. He'd colic, for sure.

Clipping Magician to the cross-ties, Kate grabbed a handful of rags from the tack rom. She removed his bridle and loosened his girth and rubbed off the worst of the sweat before covering him with a cooler. Then she led him outside, into the ring, and started walking him out.

Minutes later, an ambulance roared by, sirens wailing, followed by a police car and Mrs. Piretti's black Range Rover.

Kate watched them disappear in a cloud of dust. How long did she have to fudge up a bunch of excuses before Holly got back and began asking questions Kate didn't want to answer?

6

KATE WAS IN MAGICIAN'S STALL, settling him down, when she heard cars coming back. Wheels crunched on gravel. Doors opened and banged shut. Voices reached her — Holly, Sue's mother, and a man, probably one of the cops. Then, silence. Kate pictured them pulling Holly's chair from the back of Mrs. Piretti's car, unfolding it, and helping Holly get comfortable. In a matter of minutes, Holly would be in the barn. Kate crossed her fingers that she'd be alone. Facing Holly would be bad enough. She didn't want an audience as well.

Minutes passed.

Nothing.

Was Holly coming inside or not?

Finally, she heard wheels, a rhythmic click as Holly's chair clattered down the cement aisle. Kate held perfectly still, hardly daring to breathe. The stall door slid open, and Magician whickered with recognition.

"Kate McGregor, you're a liar," Holly said, her voice loaded with anger. "Why did you tell us you couldn't ride?"

Kate opened her mouth, but nothing came out.

"You pretended to be afraid," Holly went on, sounding miserable as well as angry. "But you weren't, and I want to know why."

Kate's carefully rehearsed speech went down the drain. "I'm sorry, really sorry, but —" She gulped. "How's Sue? What did the medics say?"

"They don't think it's anything serious," Holly said. She nodded toward Magician. "And when you've finished with my horse, meet me in the tack room." Then she jerked her chair around and wheeled herself out of the stall.

Heart thumping like sneakers in a dryer, Kate stared at the angry space where Holly had been. Now what? Tell her the truth, or pack it in and go back to Aunt Marion's cottage? Magician nudged her with his nose. She wrapped her arms around his warm, velvety neck and wished she could stay in his stall forever. If only she could let go of her guilt. Why was she punishing herself? Hadn't Mrs. Mueller punished her enough by banishing her from the barn? And what about her old friends — the ones who'd loved Black Magic as much as she had? How they must hate her.

Stalling for time, Kate checked Magician's water bucket, adjusted his cooler, and fed him another flake of hay. Then she plucked up what was left of her courage and went to join Holly in the tack room.

* * *

"Well?" Holly said. Her eyes glittered with tears. One trickled down her cheek, and Kate had to stop herself from leaning over and wiping it off. Instead, she cleared a space for herself on a tack trunk, sat down hard, and buried her face in her hands.

"Right now," Holly said, "I think I hate you as much as I hate Angela Dean. Maybe more. At least I know what she's like. I know what to expect, but you —" Her voice cracked. "I thought you were my friend."

"I am your friend, but —"

"So why did you lie?" Holly said.

"Because I couldn't face the truth."

"That's a cop-out," Holly said. "You're talking in riddles. Tell me why you lied, or I'm going home." She grabbed the wheels of her chair and began to turn away.

"Okay, I'll tell you," Kate said. It was now or never. She couldn't keep it bottled up any longer. That ride on Magician had shaken things loose, brought it all back.

Holly swiveled to face her.

"But before I do," Kate rushed on. "You have to promise me one thing."

"What?"

"Don't tell your mother."

"Why?"

"You'll understand after I explain," Kate said. "Please."

Holly hesitated. "Okay, I promise, but this better be good."

Kate picked up a crop and tapped it against her leg. "I used to ride at a place called Sandpiper Stables. Their best horse was a Trakehner named Black Magic. I helped with his training. He'd once been a jumper, but his dressage was so good, we competed in combined training events." She took a deep breath. This was tougher than she'd expected. "Mrs. Mueller had big plans for Magic. She hoped we'd make it all the way to Young Riders."

Holly whistled through her teeth. "Heady stuff."

Kate nodded miserably, thinking of all she had lost.

"Go on," Holly said, her voice softer.

"Magic was an escape artist. He got out of every stall, every field we put him in. He'd either undo the latch or else he'd jump out. I worked at the stables in return for free lessons. One night, after I'd fed all the horses, Magic got out."

"Didn't you lock him in?" Holly asked.

"Of course," Kate replied. "But it didn't always work."

"So, what happened?"

"He broke into the feed room and gorged on sweet feed," Kate said. "Mrs. Mueller found him and called the vet, but it was too late. He colicked and died the next morning."

"Oh, no!"

Kate burst into tears.

Holly pulled a tissue from her pocket. "Here."

"Thanks." Kate wiped her eyes. She hadn't bawled like this in ages. Not even when Mrs. Mueller accused her of killing the barn's best horse. She'd kept her tears for Black Magic private, far away from the boarders and other kids who rode at the stables. They'd stared and whispered the next morning as Kate collected her chaps and helmet, her spare boots and grooming box from the tack room, and left the barn without looking back.

Holly sighed. "Maybe it wasn't your fault."

"Of course, it was." Kate sniffed. "It was my responsibility to make sure his door was locked, and I blew it. I was the last one there, and I —"

"Are you sure?" Holly said. "I mean, couldn't someone else have checked the horses *after* you left and forgotten to lock Magic's door?"

"How I wish," Kate said. "But Mrs. Mueller said nobody came to the barn after me."

"It was an accident," Holly said. "A stupid, horrible accident."

Kate shook her head. "I was in a rush to get home that night. Dad had a meeting to attend, and I had a ton of homework."

"But I still don't get it," Holly said. "Why did you tell us you couldn't ride? Why pretend to be scared of horses?"

"Because I couldn't face a horse — *any* horse —

after that," Kate said. "I was hoping the job here wouldn't involve coming to the barn; but when it did, I had to think of an excuse."

"Why didn't you tell us the truth?"

"Would your Mom have hired a horse killer?"

Holly winced.

"See," Kate said.

"But you didn't kill him," Holly insisted.

"How do you know?"

"Because you're too careful. You always check things. Look how you raced back home yesterday to make sure Mom had turned off the coffee pot." Holly paused. "And this morning, we were half way to the barn when you insisted Mom had left the garden hose filling the pool."

"Well, she hadn't," Kate said, blushing.

"Doesn't matter," Holly said. "The thing is, you'd never have forgotten to double-check that stall door."

"Tell that to Mrs. Mueller," Kate said.

"I wish I could."

"Just promise not to tell your mother, okay?"

"Oh, all right," Holly said, sounding reluctant. "But I think *you* ought to tell Mom. She trusts you; and I bet if you explain, she'll understand."

"No, she won't."

"Well, *I* don't think it was you fault."

Kate let out a sigh. "Thanks."

"I just wish Mom could see you ride," Holly said. "From what I saw when you took off with my horse, you looked pretty good." She paused. "Mom could use you on the team, especially if Sue's not fit enough to compete."

More guilt shot through Kate. Now she felt even worse. Without four riders, Timber Ridge might have to withdraw from next week's Hampshire Classic, and she knew how much Liz was counting on a successful show. Maybe Sue would be okay. It wasn't as if she'd broken any bones. All she had was a black eye and a face full of scratches. Kate glanced at her legs. Tiny bruises mottled her skin from knee to ankle, thanks to her wild ride on Magician. Had Holly told Sue and Mrs. Piretti about it?

She asked.

Holly shook her head. "Nobody knows but you, me, and my horse." She paused. "Well? Are you going to tell Mom or not?"

Kate hesitated. She owed this much to Liz. "If Sue can't ride, then I will."

* * *

a horse show with Liz, helping out with the younger kids, and Denise and Angela always spent Saturday afternoons playing tennis at the club.

She'd have the place to herself.

The horses had been turned out to graze in the back paddock. They stood beneath a grove of trees in the far corner, head to tail, swishing flies off one another.

Kate climbed the fence and straddled it, the way she once had at Sandpiper Stables. Someone's tractor rumbled in the distance, and she could see brightly dressed mountain bikers riding up and down the ski trails on Timber Ridge Mountain. In the short time she'd been with the Chapmans, she'd come to love this place even better than home. She and her father lived in a condo in Connecticut. No animals allowed except for her dad's dead butterflies. If only he'd agree to move up here. Trouble was, he needed to be close to his university.

Fumbling in her pocket for a carrot, she called out to Magician. He looked up, ears pricked.

"Come on," Kate called out. "Here's your carrot."

He took two steps and then halted.

"Can't say I blame him," said an icy voice behind her. "Why should he trust you? You're a horse killer."

As Kate pushed Holly's wheelchair out of the barn, neither of them saw a figure, standing in the shadows. Another pair of eyes had seen Kate jump Magician over the back gate — pale blue eyes that were now angry and dangerous.

And jealous.

Angela let out a gasp of anger as she emerged from her hiding place in Liz's office. Just think! If she hadn't stuck around to listen, she'd never have discovered Kate McGregor's terrible secret.

A horse killer.

How interesting. How incredibly interesting.

Angela's brow furrowed. She had a serious problem. If Liz Chapman saw Kate in action, she'd put her on the team, never mind if Sue could ride or not. And that would never do because then Kate would take Angela's place.

Despite what she told her mother, Angela knew she was the team's weakest rider. But she needed the team. She needed those blue ribbons.

They made her mother happy.

How best to handle this? Tell her mother, and have Kate banished from the barn right away? That was one possibility. But there was another one, a far better one.

Angela smiled.

Her position on the team was secure. No way would she lose out to a nobody like Kate McGregor.

* * *

"Okay," Holly said. "Let's go over this again, just to be sure we have our stories straight. We both have to say the same thing."

Kate smiled at Holly's anxious face. That morning, while lying by the pool, they'd decided on a compromise. If Kate had to take Sue's place on the team, they wouldn't tell Liz the truth about Black Magic. They'd give her another reason for Kate's having lied.

"You had a dreadful accident, and you were scared stiff," Holly said. "Let's see." She frowned. "You were riding a horse . . . quick, think of a name for me."

"Seabiscuit?"

"Be serious."

"How about Webster?" Kate suggested. "He was the first pony I ever rode."

"Good," Holly replied. "Now, you were riding this horse, Webster, and he slipped going over a jump. You fell off, hit the rails, and he landed on top of you."

"Was I killed?"

"No, stupid, but you were hurt. Really bad. A concussion. You lost your memory."

"Sure, and I wandered around the woods in a daze for two months and just happened to end up in Vermont working for you." Kate shook her head. "Come on, Holly. We've got to do better than this. Liz won't believe a word of it. Why don't we just tell her I had a bad fall, lost my nerve, and quit riding forever? She'll buy that, won't she?"

"Sounds okay to me," Holly said.

"Let's hope we won't have to use it," Kate said. So far, things were looking good for Sue. She was home from the hospital with nothing more than cuts and bruises and a massive black eye. She'd called earlier to say she'd be back in the saddle Monday morning. Kate was hugely relieved. She didn't want to ride; but much to her surprise, she found herself wanting to visit the barn . . . on her own.

"Go ahead," Holly said. "I need to finish this." She waved yet another horse book in the air. "It's getting exciting."

After making sure Holly had everything she needed, Kate changed into jeans and sneakers and set off for the barn. With luck, nobody would be there. Robin was at

7

KATE PANICKED. In a flash, her mind shot back in time. She was listening to Mrs. Mueller yelling at her, over and over again. *You killed my horse.*

No, no, I didn't.

Oh, yes, you did.

Kate whirled around. "What are *you* doing here?"

"I could ask you the same thing," Angela drawled. "I'm surprised you have the nerve to come anywhere near our horses."

How on earth had Angela found out?

"Maybe I should have my mother call Mrs. Mueller and get the full story," Angela said. She leaned against the fence and twirled a piece of grass between her fingers.

"What did you —?" Kate stumbled over the words. "How did you —?"

Angela smirked. "I saw you jump the gate on Magician." She paused and her mouth twisted into a thin, crooked line. "I must say, even I was fooled by your dumb playacting. But after what you told Holly, I'm not surprised you had to keep it quiet."

"It was an accident."

"I doubt it," Angela snapped. "You admitted you were in a rush. You didn't check that stall door, yet you knew that horse was good at escaping. You're sloppy and unreliable, and you killed a valuable horse."

Kate jumped off the fence and took a step toward Angela. Any closer, and she'd lose control and smack her in the mouth.

"I wonder what Liz would do if she discovered she had a liar *and* a horse killer living in her house," Angela went on. "My mother really wouldn't approve of that. She's very fussy about the kind of people who're hired to do the work around here." Her eyes narrowed into slits. "And that's all you are, you know. Just the hired help, even if you do pretend to be Holly's friend."

Kate thought about Liz's worry over having her contract renewed. If Mrs. Dean got wind of this, she'd force Liz to fire her. Or worse, she'd fire Liz as well. No

way could Kate have this on her conscience. There
wasn't room for any more guilt.

With a calm she didn't feel, Kate looked the other
girl squarely in the eye. "All right, Angela. You win.
What do you want?"

"Simple," Angela said. "You keep pretending to be
scared of horses, and I won't tell my mother you killed
that horse."

Kate clenched her fists and bit back the torrent of
angry words that surged up her throat. She wanted to
scream at Angela, to wipe the smug look off her face,
but things were already bad enough. No sense in making them worse.

"You're not to tell Liz about this, either," Angela
said.

"And if I refuse?"

"Then you're toast," Angela said. "And so is Liz
Chapman." She glanced at her watch. "You have a
minute to decide."

A minute. An hour. What difference did it make?

"All right," Kate said, feeling as if someone had
punched her in the gut. "You've got what you wanted,
now go away and leave me alone."

"Whatever," Angela said and sauntered off.

* * *

69

"But that's . . . that's *blackmail*," Holly cried after Kate told her about Angela's threat. "She can't get away with this. I'm going to tell Mom."

"No!" Kate said. "You mustn't."

"Why not?"

"Because she'd fire me," Kate said. "She wouldn't have a choice. It'd be that or else lose her own job."

Holly narrowed her eyes. "So, what's to stop Angela from ratting on you anyway?"

"She won't."

"You're dreaming," Holly said. "It'll be all over the barn in a nanosecond."

Kate shook her head. "I don't think so."

"Why not?"

"Angela *likes* having me here. I'm someone she can kick around because she knows I won't fight back. She's got me exactly where she wants me." Kate shrugged and looked at Holly. "At least she won't be picking on you any more."

Holly scowled. "But there's got to be *something* we can do."

Kate shook her head. "There isn't, so stop worrying."

"So what *do* we do?"

"Nothing," Kate said. "Absolutely nothing. Sue will ride Magician in the Classic, and things will go on the same as before. You'll take lessons on Plug, I'll cringe and hide from the horses, and Angela will make fun of me."

"But what if Sue *can't* ride?" Holly said. "Suppose her —?"

"She'll be fine," Kate assured her. "You heard what she said. The doctor told her she could start riding again on Monday."

* * *

By the time Liz returned from the horse show, Kate had convinced Holly to keep quiet. Good thing, too. Liz didn't look as if she could handle any more bad news. Her face was pale, her lips a thin line, and she had dark circles beneath her eyes.

"Bad day, huh, Mom?" Holly asked.

Liz kicked off her boots and collapsed on the couch. "The pits," she said. "Just promise me one thing, okay?"

"What?"

"Next time I schedule a show, remind me not to put Laura Gardner and Marcia Dean in the same classes."

Holly pulled a face. "Sure, but why?"

"Because they tried to kill each other."

"Seriously?"

"The apple bobbing race was the worst," Liz said.

"I *loved* that event," Holly said. "Which ponies were they riding?"

"Snowball and Plug," Liz said. "Everything started off fine. The girls raced their ponies to the buckets, jumped off, and bobbed for the apples. But then Marcia let go of Snowball's reins, and he stuck his head in Laura's bucket and swiped her apple. So Laura whacked Marcia with her crop, and then Plug stepped on Laura's foot."

Holly started to giggle. So did Kate.

"It went downhill from there," Liz said, running a hand through her hair. "The truck had a flat, so I had to change the tire; and then the ponies refused to load on the trailer. The girls were still squabbling, and I was about to give them a time-out when Mrs. Dean stormed up and insisted I give Angela extra lessons this week so she'll win the individual medal at the Hampshire."

"But she's not good enough," Holly said.

Liz sighed. "I know, but she could be if she practiced. She's got a great horse."

"Will you give her the lessons?"

"I don't have a choice," Liz said, yawning. "I should've told Mrs. Dean to bribe the judges instead. It'd work better than lessons. Angela hardly ever shows up, anyway." She stood up and stretched. "I'm going for a shower. If I don't come out, it means I fell asleep. Just toss a blanket over me, okay?" She paused at the door. "Any word from Sue?"

Holly grinned. "She's fine, and she'll be at the barn first thing Monday morning."

Liz sagged with relief. "Thank goodness."

After Liz had disappeared, Kate asked Holly about the show.

"It's kind of like a three-day event," Holly said. "Dressage, cross-country, and jumping. But the teams are judged on stable management as well."

"Will the team win?"

"They'd better, or Mom's contract might not be renewed."

"Did they compete last year?"

Holly nodded. "Third place. Mom was thrilled, but Mrs. Dean had a fit. She yelled at Angela for not winning the individual prize, then reamed Mom out for her team's shoddy performance."

"Third isn't shoddy," Kate said.

"Try telling that to Mrs. Dean."

"But why does she care?" Kate said. "What's in it for her?"

"Gives her something to show off about," Holly said. "She loves impressing her fancy friends with Angela's trophies."

Kate groaned. "Typical horse-show mother."

"And don't let on to Mom," Holly went on, "but Robin Shapiro's mother found out that Mrs. Dean has promised the homeowners' association they'll have a winning team this year."

"That's really stupid," Kate said. "Anybody could win. Riders fall off and get hurt, horses go lame. You never know what's going to happen."

"Yeah, I know," Holly said. "But Mrs. Dean hasn't got a clue. She knows nothing about horses except what Angela tells her. So, of course, Angela has convinced her mother that she'll win the medal and the team will get the challenge cup this year." Holly looked down at her hands. "I guess it's her only defense."

"What do you mean?"

"Angela's mother only loves her when she's winning trophies and blue ribbons," Holly said grimly.

Kate shuddered. "Makes me feel almost sorry for her."

"Hey," Holly said. "I wouldn't go *that* far."

❊ ❊ ❊

The next morning, after Liz left for the barn and Kate had gone to visit her aunt, Holly grabbed a book and her cell phone and wheeled herself into the backyard. The long grass jammed her wheels and made it hard to maneuver. Mom hadn't mowed in over two weeks, but she hadn't had a spare minute to do it. Holly couldn't even remember the last time her mother had taken a day off. If it weren't for this stupid chair, Holly thought, she'd be able to fire up the tractor and mow the lawn herself. This was something she and her dad used to do. She'd sit in front of him, and he'd let her steer. Sometimes, they made crazy patterns in the grass.

Tears pricked at Holly's eyes. Why did he have to die? Why couldn't she have a dad like the other kids? Then she thought about Kate, who didn't have a mother. From the sounds of it, she didn't have much of a father, either.

The phone rang and startled her.

"Holly, it's Sue. Is your mom there?"

Boy, she sounded awful, as if she'd been crying "No, she's at the barn." Holly gripped her cell phone tighter. "Sue, what's wrong?"

"I've been grounded."

"Why? What did you do this time?" Holly said. Sue was always getting into scrapes and making her mother mad.

Sue groaned. "I fell off a horse. Remember?"

"But the doc said you were fine."

"He looked at my x-rays again and changed his mind," Sue said. "Apparently, I've had a concussion, and now I'm supposed to take it easy. No running, no skateboarding, and no riding for at least three weeks."

"But Sue," Holly said. "The Hampshire starts on Friday."

"I know," Sue wailed. "And I can't go."

"But —"

"Look, I gotta go back to bed. But tell Liz for me, okay?" Sue said. "Tell her I'm sorry." She hung up.

Stunned by the news, Holly dropped the phone in her lap. With Sue Piretti out of action, the team was in trouble. They needed four riders, and there wasn't anyone else good enough to take her place.

Or was there?

Would Kate honor her promise?

Yes, but only if they figured out a way to remove the teeth from Angela's threat.

8

HOLLY PUNCHED THE AIR with her fist. For once, she could do something to help, and she didn't need two functioning legs to pull it off. Feeling useful for the first time in months, Holly snatched up her phone and dialed her mother's cell. It went to voice mail, so she called the barn's number.

One of the kids answered, and it was several minutes before her mother's voice, distracted and tense, came on the line. "Holly, I hope this is important, because if not, then —"

"Mom, you have to come home. Right now," Holly said.

"Are you all right?"

"I'm fine," Holly said. "But Sue isn't. She's been grounded."

There was a brief silence.

"Grounded?"

"The doc says she has a concussion. He won't let her ride."

Liz groaned. "Oh, no. *Now* what do I do?"

"That's what I need to talk to you about," Holly said. "But not on the phone. You've got to come home, now." She paused, then added to herself, *before Kate gets back.*

"Okay," her mother said. "I'll be there in ten minutes, and this had better be good."

Ten minutes, Holly thought. That would give her just enough time. She zoomed up the back ramp, shot through the kitchen, and raced down the hall toward her room. Good thing the doorways in this house were wide enough for a speeding wheelchair.

Herds of wild horses galloped in slow motion across her laptop's screen. Holly touched the keyboard, and the horses disappeared. She logged onto the web.

What was it called? Sand Hill? Sandy Hook? No, it was a bird. Seagull? Siskin? *Think, Holly, think.* She was about to reach for her Audubon guide, when she remembered.

Sandpiper. Sandpiper Stables.

Holly typed the name into Google, and dozens of

results came up — horse farms and riding stables from all over the country.

She narrowed her search to New England and then to Connecticut.

One hit.

"Bingo!" Holly cried, as pictures of dressage horses and show jumpers filled the screen beneath the farm's name. She scrolled back and forth until she found the phone number, then grabbed a pencil and wrote it down.

Now all she had to do was wait till Mom showed up.

Holly wheeled herself into the kitchen and watched the clock. Should she go ahead and call Sandpiper Stables herself? No, it'd be better for Mom to call. Mrs. Mueller didn't sound like the sort of person who'd listen to a kid. Look at the way she treated poor Kate.

Half an hour later, Holly's anxiety was about to boil over when her mother raced through the door.

"Whatever's on your mind," Liz said, "it'll have to wait. I've got to call Mrs. Dean and tell her I'm pulling out of the competition. We can't compete without Sue."

"We can," Holly said. "I found a replacement."

"You'd better not be thinking about yourself," Liz said, "because I'm in no mood for jokes."

"Not me," Holly said. "Kate."

Liz stared at her, openmouthed. "What?"

"Mom, Kate can ride," Holly said. "She's amazing, and she can take Sue's place."

Grabbing a chair, Liz sat down. "You'd better explain," she said. "You're not making any sense."

By the time Holly got through telling her about Black Magic's death and Kate's ride on Magician, Liz's expression had cycled through dismay, anger, and amazement. "Poor Kate," she said. "How horrible for her."

"Mom, you don't believe it was her fault, do you?"

Liz shook her head. "No."

Holly let out her breath, unaware she'd been holding it.

"Kate's a responsible girl," Liz said. "I can't imagine her *not* checking that stall door." She tapped her fingers on the table. "I bet you anything there was someone else in that horse's stall *after* her that night."

"That's what I think," Holly said.

"But how do we find out," Liz said.

"Call Mrs. Mueller."

Her mother raised an eyebrow. "And I suppose you already have the number?"

"Yup."

Liz stood up. "I should've known."

Holly read out the number. "Don't get your hopes up," Liz said, punching it into her cell. "It's Sunday, and I doubt anyone will be around. They're probably off at a show."

"But, Mom, surely *someone's* there. I bet there's a —"

Liz held up her hand for Holly to be quiet. "Mrs. Mueller? I'm Liz Chapman. I'm calling from Vermont, about Kate McGregor, and —"

While her mother paced the kitchen, Holly bit her lip and tried to guess what was being said on the other end of the phone. But it was impossible. Her mom just frowned a few times, nodded her head, and said things like, "Are you sure?" and "How awful for you." Just when Holly thought she'd burst with curiosity, her mother's face broke into a smile.

"What did she say? Was it Kate's fault?" Holly said.

Liz hung up and, for a second or two, said nothing. "No."

Holly shrieked. She leaned forward and almost fell

out of her chair. Liz grabbed her shoulders. "Be careful."

"What happened?" Holly said.

"Black Magic did get out of his stall and into the feed room, just like Kate said. When he colicked and died, Mrs. Mueller was frantic. She blamed Kate, and now she feels terrible because it wasn't Kate's fault."

"Why didn't Mrs. Mueller tell her?" Holly asked.

"Because by the time they figured out what had happened, Kate had come here and her father was in Brazil. Nobody knew how to reach either of them."

"So tell me what she said."

Liz dropped her phone on the table and sat down. "Apparently, they sent Black Magic's body up to Tufts Veterinary Center for an autopsy," she said.

"Why?"

"Insurance. He was a valuable horse. They had to prove, without question, what killed him."

"And?" Holly said.

"Not colic," Liz replied. "Cancer. A tumor the size of a baseball in his intestines. He was a walking time bomb. He could've died at any time. All that sweet feed didn't help, but it didn't kill him."

"But Mom, this won't make Kate feel any better.

She's still going to blame herself for not checking that stall door."

"Wait, there's more," Liz said. "A couple of months later, one of Mrs. Mueller's riding students confessed."

"Confessed?"

Liz nodded. "Apparently this girl, Janet, had been in the stables after Kate that night. Black Magic was out of water, and she filled his bucket but —"

"Forgot to lock his stall door," Holly finished.

"You got it."

"So why did Janet let Kate take the blame?"

"She was scared. And when Kate disappeared and nobody knew how to find her, Janet decided to keep her mouth shut."

"The rotten little coward," Holly said.

"But when Janet heard the results of the autopsy, she realized it wasn't her fault and decided to own up," Liz explained

"Mom," Holly said, "you know what this means, don't you?"

"Yes. Kate can stop feeling guilty, and we can invite her to be part of the team." Liz grasped Holly's hand. "I hope you're not exaggerating about Kate and the way she rode Magician."

"I'm not," Holly said. "She's terrific." She thought about telling her mother that Kate had jumped the back gate, but decided not to risk it. Mom would have a bird.

"In that case," Liz said. "You must bring her to the barn the minute she gets home. I can't wait to see her ride."

And I can't wait to see Angela's face when she hears the truth, Holly thought, as her mother left the kitchen and went back to work.

* * *

Two hours later, Holly sat in her mother's office, barely able to contain her excitement, while Liz told Kate the good news. At first, Kate didn't appear to believe her; but once it finally sank in, she began to cry.

Liz hugged her. "It's all over now," she said. "I'm sorry about Black Magic, but it wasn't your fault. Mrs. Mueller said to tell you there's an open door waiting, if you ever want to go back."

Kate sniffed and wiped her nose on her sleeve. "Are you sure? I mean, I'm not dreaming, am I?"

"Of course not," Liz said. She gripped Kate by the shoulders. "Holly's impressed with your riding. So why don't we saddle up Magician, and you can impress me as well."

"Mom, what're you going to tell Angela?"

"The truth would be best."

"Then you'd better wear a bullet-proof vest," Holly said, "or carry a white flag."

Liz laughed. "No need for dramatics, here," she said. "I'll just have a quiet word with Angela and set her straight, and then I'll tell Mrs. Dean that Kate will be taking Sue's place on the team." She looked at Kate. "That is, of course, if you want to."

"Try and stop me," Kate said, grinning.

* * *

Liz and Holly watched from the center of the ring as Kate, wearing Robin's helmet and a pair of Liz's old boots, put Magician through his paces. How different from their wild ride through the woods. This time, she held him lightly in her hands as if afraid he might break. With gentle pressure, she drove him forward, into the bit, and asked for extensions and half-halts, circles at the trot and canter.

How smooth he was.

Magician glided through transitions, performed a

flawless shoulder-in, and took her breath away with a hand-gallop down the center of the arena.

Liz adjusted the cavallettis. "Warm up over these," she called out. "Then try the cross-rails. After that, take the brush jump and the parallel bars."

Magician needed no encouragement. Ears pricked, he gathered himself up and flew over the brightly colored fences as if they were no bigger than the toy jumps in Holly's bedroom. At Liz's command, Kate reversed direction and took the jumps again, adding the double oxer for good measure.

Flushed with excitement, she rode up to Liz. It was time to find out how she'd done.

Liz smiled. "Holly was right. You're good. *Very* good."

"Better than me?" Holly said.

"Maybe."

"I *told* you," Holly said, grinning. "So, do we have a chance this weekend?"

"Don't see why not," Liz said, running her hands down Magician's forelegs. She straightened and looked up at Kate. "This means you have a huge amount of work to do, and only four days to do it in."

Kate grinned. "I know."

"Think you can handle it?" Holly said.

She was about to reply when a movement caught her eye. She turned and there, leaning against the rails, were Angela and Denise.

"Hold onto your hats," Holly muttered. "The cat's about to jump out of the bag."

"Liz, I need to talk to you," Angela yelled. "Right now."

Kate stared at them. Dressed in white, Angela and Denise carried tennis racquets and balls. Why weren't they riding instead? From what Kate had seen, they both needed all the practice they could get. Denise rarely posted on the correct diagonal, and Angela kept such a tight rein that Skywalker constantly fought the bit.

Liz walked up to them. She ducked beneath the fence, gestured toward the barn, and led both girls inside.

Kate sighed. "I sure don't envy your mom."

"Neither do I," Holly said. "We've got four days to get ready, and I don't trust Angela to behave herself."

"But what on earth can she do now?" Kate said.

Magician lowered his head, and Holly rubbed his nose. "I don't know, but we'd better be on guard."

9

AT TEN THE NEXT MORNING, Liz gathered her students in the tack room and announced a change in plans for the Hampshire Classic.

"As you all know, Sue had an accident and can't ride," she said. "Kate McGregor will be taking her place."

There was a collective gasp from the riders. None of them, except Denise and Angela, had seen Kate ride Magician. The little kids giggled and nudged one another. Two girls who'd just begun riding and were still at the walk-trot stage looked at Kate with curiosity. Robin Shapiro gave Kate a high five.

"Way to go," she said.

Kate felt herself flush with excitement — or was it

foreboding. She risked a quick glance at Angela. The return look had enough venom to strip paint.

"We'll be competing with Denise, Angela, Robin, and Kate," Liz said, handing out rules and schedules for the three-day competition. "We all have a lot of work to do, and I expect everyone to cooperate. This means practice twice a day, and anyone who skips will be —"

"Booted from the team?" Denise murmured, just loud enough to be heard.

Eyes wide, Angela looked around. "So, where *are* the spare riders, anyway?" she said, looking straight at Holly. "Who do we have for backup in case someone else gets hurt?"

Holly clutched Kate's arm. "I may have to kill them," she said through clenched teeth. "Why do they have to make fun of Mom's hard work?"

"Before you interrupted," Liz said, fixing Denise with a look, "I was about to say that anyone who skips practice will find themselves cleaning extra tack."

"That'll be the day," Holly whispered. "Angela *never* cleans tack."

"Why should I bother?" Angela drawled, as she and Denise headed for the door. "It only gets dirty again."

* * *

Kate had never worked so hard in her life, not even for Mrs. Mueller. But she happily endured sore muscles and stiff legs as Liz coached her and Magician.

There was so much to learn and so little time. Dressage was the easiest, but only because Magician was responsive and well-trained. Kate memorized the test and practiced riding it until she could do it in her sleep. Her father had once asked her to explain dressage. Kate told him it was like compulsory figures in ice-skating, a series of maneuvers to show the judges you really did know what you were doing. He seemed to have a better understanding after that. Not that he came to any of her events, though. They always seemed to coincide with a field trip or a lecture he couldn't miss.

Magician excelled on the cross-country course. His powerful legs ate up the distance, and he soared over the jumps like an enormous bird. At first, he was so eager to run that Kate had a hard time holding him back. He wanted to race.

In the riding ring, Liz set up a jump course similar to the one at the previous year's Hampshire Classic, and Kate joined the rest of the team as they practiced for the last time.

"Magician will make mincemeat out of those," Holly declared. And, she was right. One by one, Magician leaped over the brightly colored obstacles. All Kate had to do was steer him in the right direction.

"Okay, kids. That's enough," Liz said, after her team had jumped the course three times without a problem. "We're as ready as we'll ever be. No riding to-morrow."

Angela and Denise cheered.

"You'll be cleaning tack and grooming horses in-stead," Liz said. "And make sure your riding clothes are clean and pressed. No broken buckles, no missing buttons. Black hunt jackets and buff breeches for dres-sage and jumping, team t-shirts and cap covers for the cross-country." She paused. "And don't let me catch any of you without a regulation helmet and body pro-tector."

* * *

The day before the show dawned gray and gloomy. Overcast skies promised rain before nightfall. But Kate's spirits were anything but gray when she and Holly arrived at the barn. Robin's mare, Chantilly, stood in the wash stall while her owner scrubbed at the grass stains on her belly. Denise, with a sour look on her face, rubbed soap into her saddle. Skywalker, obviously bored, chewed on his stall door. His mane and tail were full of knots, his coat dull with mud. There was no sign of his owner.

While Holly took Magician's bridle apart for cleaning, Kate groomed the big black horse. He'd rolled in the dirt and his coat was filthy, but she didn't care. Grooming him was part of the fun. She discovered his ticklish spots and curried them till he curled his lip with pleasure. Then she switched to the soft body brush and, with wide, sweeping strokes, polished his ebony coat till it shone.

"Should I braid his mane?" she asked Holly.

"Yes," Holly said. "There's a box of elastics in the tack room. I'll get them. Need anything else?"

"Hoof dressing," Kate said, "and a cooler. I'm going to cover him up so he won't get dirty if he lies down."

When Holly returned, Kate went to work on Magician's mane. First, she separated it into small bunches and secured them with elastics. Then, one by one, she braided the bunches, folded them under twice, and fastened them with more elastics. By the time she finished,

Magician had fifteen knobby little braids along the crest of his neck. She had to stand on a box to braid his forelock; and when she had finished, Holly declared he'd never looked spiffier.

"Can't say the same about us, though," Kate said, wiping the sweat from her face. Horse hair and mud covered her t-shirt, wisps of hay stuck to her hair, and shavings clung to her legs like burrs on a blanket. Holly didn't look any better. She had streaks of saddle soap up both arms and a glob of silver polish on her nose.

Kate reached for the bridle Holly had cleaned. Soft and smooth. So was the saddle. The stirrups gleamed, the bit and buckles shone. She was going to look terrific in the show ring: clean tack, clean horse, and a riding outfit they'd cobbled together at the last minute — Susan's hunt jacket and body protector, Robin's spare helmet, and Liz's breeches and boots. Holly donated her rat-catcher shirt.

Kate was all set to go.

But her good mood vanished the minute Angela showed up, pristine and neat, not a hair out of place. No wrinkles marred the surface of her tailored pink shirt, and the creases in her tan slacks looked sharp enough to cut butter.

"Your horse is a mess," Holly said. "Better get moving."

Angela sniffed. "Where's Liz? I need to speak with her." She glanced at Kate, then at Magician. "Nice braids, but it's really too bad," she said. "All that hard work for nothing."

Kate's stomach lurched. *What was Angela up to now?*

"Mom's in her office," Holly said, her voice tight as a drum. "She's busy."

"Not too busy to see this." Angela waved a small book beneath Holly's nose.

"What's that?" Holly said.

Angela smirked. "You'll see."

By the time Liz emerged from her office, all her students were gathered in the aisle outside Magician's stall. Laura Gardner and Marcia Dean took turns balancing on a bucket. The two new girls sat on a tack trunk and looked up at Kate, whose heart was beating so fast that she was scared to open her mouth in case it jumped out.

"All right, Angela," Liz said. "Now you've got everyone's attention, you'd better tell me what's going on."

With a malicious gleam in her eye, Angela handed Liz the book. "This is the Homeowners' Association Rules and Bylaws," she said. "Take a look at page twenty-one. My mother circled the important paragraph." Then she folded her arms and looked directly at Kate. "Turns out you can't ride after all."

"Mom," Holly cried. "Where does it say that?"

Liz sighed. "I'm afraid Angela might be right."

Kate gasped and turned away, fighting back tears.

"I don't believe it," Holly said. "Mom, tell her she's wrong."

"I can't," Liz said, scanning the page again. "There's a rule here that says any person representing Timber Ridge in a sporting event must be a resident."

"But, Mom," Holly protested, "Kate *is* a resident. She lives with us."

"Kate only works here," Angela said, her eyes flashing with triumph. "She's the hired help, and she's not eligible to ride for the team."

Holly whirled her chair to face Angela, almost knocking her over. "There won't *be* a team if Kate doesn't ride," she said. "We have to have four riders."

Kate held her breath. Holly was right. Maybe it wasn't all over.

"Wrong, Holly Chapman," Angela said. "A team can have three members if they want. Only the top three scores from each team count."

Crash!

There was a clatter as Marcia Dean fell off her bucket and landed on top of Laura. Liz, still reading the rule book, didn't appear to have noticed them. The girls scrambled to their feet and ran off, swatting one another with saddle pads.

"Mom," Holly said. "*Do* we need four riders?"

"Technically, no, we don't," Liz said slowly. She ran a hand through her hair, now sticking up in all directions. "But it's better to have four. Nobody ever competes with only three. Too risky. You never know when something's going to go wrong."

"Nothing will go wrong," Angela said. "And we don't need Kate McGregor to win the trophy."

Liz tucked the book in her pocket. "Angela, that's quite enough," she said. "Don't you have a horse to groom, tack to clean?"

"I've got a great idea," Angela said. "Why don't we hire Kate to do it for us? I mean, if she can't ride in the competition, it seems a shame not to let her come along anyway. She might be quite useful. I'm sure she'd love to help out." She looked directly at Kate. "Wouldn't you?"

"Leave Kate alone," Liz said, handing Angela a curry comb. "Go and clean up your horse. If he's not spotless and braided by six o'clock tonight, you won't be on the team either."

Without meeting anyone's eyes, Kate slipped into Magician's stall. She rubbed his ears, touched his neat little braids, and kissed his soft, velvety nose. No point in blanketing him now. It didn't matter if he got dirty or made a mess of his mane. It had all been for nothing. No way could she compete. Angela had ruined everything, just as Holly predicted she would.

10

FROM HER HIDING PLACE behind Magician, Kate heard
Liz tell the rest of the team to get busy grooming their
horses and cleaning their tack. The show was going on
without Kate. If only Liz's job didn't hinge on her team
winning blue ribbons. Winning was great, but it wasn't
everything. Watching Holly ride Plug was proof of that.
Doing your best and having fun with your horse was
way more important than collecting prizes.

Kate's disappointment gave way to anger. Fury
surged up her throat; she wanted to scream, stamp her
feet, and throw things, preferably at Angela. She eyed
the pile of manure in the corner. That would do. It'd
make a marvelous mess of Angela's pink shirt.

Outside, the wind picked up. A tree branch scraped

the window, and loose gutters banged against the wall. Rain began to pound the barn's metal roof. If this kept up, the ground would be slick with mud and leaves tomorrow. Some horses hated wet weather. Kate wondered how Magician felt about it. Would he even care? Did it matter?

"Kate, are you in here?" Holly wheeled herself into the stall.

Startled, Kate emerged from the shadows.

"Don't give up yet." Holly said.

"But the rulebook says —"

Holly frowned, then glanced over her shoulder. Angela and Denise leaned against the opposite stall, giggling and whispering to one another. Holly beckoned Kate to come closer. "Robin's mother is on the homeowners' committee," she said.

"I know," Kate replied. "So what?"

"Robin just phoned her," Holly said. "Mrs. Shapiro is going to call an emergency committee meeting."

Kate stood up straighter. "When?"

"Tonight," Holly said. "She's going to get them to change the rules."

"Can she do that?" Kate said.

Holly shrugged. "We won't know till later. Mrs. Shapiro promised to call Mom by ten o'clock."

For Holly's sake, Kate forced herself to look hopeful. But honestly, what was the use? Whatever Mrs. Shapiro proposed at the meeting, Mrs. Dean would be sure to shoot down.

* * *

Every time the phone rang, Kate and Holly jumped in unison. First, it was Sue to see if they'd heard anything yet, then Aunt Marion calling to wish Kate luck. Kate didn't tell her there was a very strong chance she wouldn't be riding. Finally, at ten-fifteen, Mrs. Shapiro called.

"Zero hour," Holly muttered.

Kate grimaced, not daring to hope for good news.

Liz gestured at the girls to be quiet.

They watched, hardly daring to breathe, as Liz nodded a couple of times. Then she smiled. "Thanks, Mrs. Shapiro." Liz listened again. "Yes, you've just made my day."

"Whoopeee!" Holly yelled. She grabbed Kate's hand and pumped it up and down.

"The committee outvoted Mrs. Dean five to one," Liz said.

"Are you serious?" Kate said.

Liz nodded. "They decided that since you live here

and work for us and not for the association, you're a resident and therefore eligible to ride." She paused. "Simple as that."

"Boy, I bet Mrs. Dean was pissed off," Holly said.

"Holly!" Liz said, smiling. "Now, let's go to bed. We have a lot to do in the next three days."

* * *

They hit the road at six on Friday morning, yawning and complaining they needed more sleep. Kate hadn't dropped off until after midnight, and now she could barely keep her eyes open.

Liz drove the stables' six-horse van, with the four horses secured in their traveling stalls. Kate and Robin sat in the front, and Holly shared the back seat with three bags of shavings. Her chair and the team's saddles, bridles, and tack trunks took up the remaining two stalls, along with bales of hay, sacks of grain, pitchforks, and two muck buckets.

Angela's face had been pinched with anger earlier that morning as she tried to get her horse into the van. Skywalker refused to load, and it wasn't till Liz took over with kind words and a carrot that he walked up the ramp. Denise's mare, Luna, didn't behave much better. Ears pinned and threatening to kick, she finally scrambled into the stall beside Skywalker. Liz closed the metal gate behind her.

Carrying a tack trunk between them, Angela and Denise had emerged from the barn with saddles and bridles hooked over their arms. They dumped them in the driveway, then ran off to join Mrs. Dean in her Mercedes.

* * *

The show grounds were alive with activity, and Kate felt the familiar excitement, the old anxieties, coming back. Competing in three-day events was a whole lot of hanging about, interrupted by moments of exhilaration and sheer terror — like the time she was seconds from victory and Black Magic fell at the last fence.

Best not to think about that.

Kate peered through the van's window. Ahead, she saw white tents with bunting and flower boxes, a small grandstand, and rows of bleachers. Flags fluttered in the breeze, and a loud, raspy voice tested the public address system. The rain had stopped some time during the night, but the footing still looked wet. Good thing the cross-country didn't begin till the next day.

They followed a stream of cars and trailers past a stall selling coffee and doughnuts and another that promised hot dogs and hamburgers later on. Behind them were two riding rings: one full of brightly colored jumps, the other bordered by a low white fence and marked off with large capital letters.

The dressage arena.

Kate gulped. She'd be riding in it soon. Did she remember the test? Would she have time to run through it once more? And had she packed her leather gloves? A pair of thick socks? Liz's boots were a bit loose.

A man wearing a Day-Glo orange vest directed them to the field reserved for team parking. Off to one side, Kate saw a cluster of low, wooden buildings — the stables. People bustled about carrying buckets and flakes of hay. Two Jack Russell terriers raced in circles, yapping and getting in everyone's way. In the distance, horses and riders warmed up in the practice ring.

The Timber Ridge horse van bumped across the field, swaying from side to side as Liz did her best to avoid potholes and ruts.

"That's the Larchwood team," Holly said, pointing at a group of horses with black-and-red blankets: two chestnuts, a flashy looking pinto, and a dark bay. All wore red halters and matching leg wraps. Their riders sported red-and-black t-shirts.

"Very chic," Robin said. "I wonder if they have personal shoppers."

Holly said, "They won last year, but we're going to beat them."

Liz gave the rival team a wide berth. "They won the year before, too, and they'll be looking for a third win this year as well. They want to keep the challenge trophy." She pulled up beneath a large maple and cut the engine.

"Okay, ladies, this is it," she said. "Let's get to work. Holly, you take care of this." She handed her a list. "Make sure we've brought everything we need. If any item is missing, I'll call Mrs. Shapiro and ask her to bring it when she comes later. Kate and Robin, unload the equipment first, then the horses."

While the girls set about their tasks, Liz went to check in at the show secretary's tent. She came back with their stall assignments and riders' numbers.

"Kate, you'll be riding last, I'm afraid," Liz said, handing her number thirty-two. "Apparently, they put all the numbers in a box and pulled them out like a lottery. Robin, you're number four. Denise is fifteen, and Angela's right before Kate, number thirty-one."

"How many teams this year, Mom?" Holly asked.

"Eight, and they each have four riders."

"And so do we," Holly muttered. "No thanks to Angela."

Liz said, "Kate, help Robin prepare for her dressage test. She'll be in the ring by nine-thirty. Denise will probably ride just before lunch, and you and Angela at about four o'clock."

That long, Kate thought. *Plenty of time to have a nervous breakdown.*

* * *

An hour flew by as Kate and Robin settled the horses into their stalls. They filled water buckets and spread fresh shavings on the floor. There was no sign of Denise or Angela, so they took care of Skywalker and Luna as well. Denise's bad-tempered liver chestnut pinned her ears when Kate latched the door.

"That mare's a menace," Holly muttered. "She doesn't deserve such a pretty name."

"Luna?" Kate said. "As in lunatic?"

"No, Luna as in Moon," Holly replied. "But they should've called her Venus."

"But that's even prettier," Kate protested.

Holly glared at the mare. "Venus, as in Venus Fly-Trap," she said. "Eats cats and small children."

Once Robin was tacked up and ready to go, she set off for the practice ring where Liz was waiting with last-minute instructions. "I'll see you guys later," Robin called over her shoulder, looking nervous.

"Break a leg," Holly said.

"Good luck," Kate added.

They were about to head for the dressage arena when Angela and Denise sauntered up. Kate had to bite her lip to keep from laughing out loud. Angela was wearing formal riding clothes and looked faintly ridiculous in her yellow vest, white breeches, and shadbelly coat. In her hands she carried a black top hat.

Talk about carrying things too far.

"Mom said buff breeches and black hunt jackets," Holly warned. "You'd better change before she catches you in this" — she stifled a laugh with her hand — "fancy dress."

Angela flicked a speck of dust from her lapel. "I'll wear whatever I want," she said, glancing at her horse. "Why didn't someone take off his leg wraps?"

"Because that's *your* job," Holly snapped. "Just as it was *your* job to unload him and put him in his stall."

Kate grabbed the handles of Holly's chair. "Come on, let's get out of here. I want to watch the dressage."

"Good idea," Angela drawled. "You might learn something."

Denise snickered.

"Ignore them," Holly warned. "Don't rise to the bait."

"I'll try," Kate said, "but it's getting harder." She pushed Holly toward the dressage arena. On the way, she asked Holly when they'd begin judging the stable management.

"I think they already have," Holly said. She pointed to a man and a woman with clipboards, walking past them toward the stable area.

"Good thing I just cleaned Magician's stall," Kate said. She parked Holly's chair beside the bleachers and sat down. The crowd applauded as a boy riding a spirited black-and-white gelding trotted into the ring. With its dished face and flagged tail, the horse looked like a half-Arabian.

"He's one of the Larchwood riders," Holly said. "He won the individual medal last year. Good, isn't he?"

Kate nodded. "Cute, too."

Holly nudged her. "Better watch out. Angela had

her eye on him at the spring show." She laughed. "So did all the other girls. You don't often see boys riding around here. They're all into mountain bikes and skateboards."

Kate watched, fascinated, as the boy on the pinto performed a brilliant test and left the ring to another round of applause. *He'll be tough to beat,* she thought. "Do they score this like a normal three-day competition?" she asked Holly as a girl on a roan mare entered the arena.

"No. They have their own peculiar system. Each rider starts with one hundred points," Holly explained. "Then points are taken away for each mistake. You know, like when a horse refuses a fence or knocks one down or messes up on the dressage test. Mom says they're really strict about stable management, too." She grinned. "I've heard rumors they'll deduct points if they find more than five flies in a horse's stall."

Kate laughed and tried to stay calm.

"Robin's next," Holly said. "Fingers crossed."

"And toes," Kate said.

Chantilly looked like a wisp of gray lace as she and her rider sailed through the required movements of the test. Kate hoped she'd do as well when her turn came.

More horses and riders competed, and the time for

Kate's dressage test grew closer and closer. Then Denise was in the ring and Luna was still in a bad mood. Her tail flicked from side to side, and her ears didn't come forward once. Kate glanced at Angela, leaning against her mother's Mercedes on the other side of the arena. She was no longer wearing the shadbelly. Liz must've put her foot down, and Kate was glad.

It was about time somebody did.

11

FEET DANGLING FREE of her stirrups, Kate sat on Magician and waited in the collecting ring, wishing she hadn't eaten that greasy hamburger for lunch — or that bag of fries, either. They rumbled around her stomach like a litter of restless rabbits. As long as they didn't come back up. Barfing on a judge would be grounds for elimination. Kate chewed at her lip. She hadn't expected to be this nervous. Then again, she hadn't expected to have the worry of Liz's job on her shoulders, either. It just wasn't fair. Why couldn't Mrs. Dean understand that winning wasn't the only thing?

In the dressage arena, Angela was riding an almost perfect test. What a surprise. The last time Kate had watched Angela practice, her hands were stiffer than broomsticks, her legs busier than windmills. Kate gave Holly a thumbs up. Holly grinned and grasped her mother's hand. Liz looked relieved, as well as pleased, and Kate was glad for her sake that Angela had pushed all the right buttons.

Angela left the ring to scattered applause. Mrs. Dean rushed up, high heels catching on clumps of turf, and demanded to know if this put Angela in the lead.

"Mom, I don't *know*," Angela snapped.

Skywalker tried to eat the fake flowers in Mrs. Dean's straw hat. She snatched it away and began firing questions at Liz. Kate watched Angela ride off toward the bleachers, where the boy from Larchwood sat with his teammates . . . all girls. Angela took off her helmet and shook out her hair. It fell to her shoulders. She looked up and spoke to the boy.

The boy glanced down at her. From his expression it was obvious he didn't have a clue who she was. He smiled, then shrugged and returned to his conversation. Angela's smile vanished. She kicked Skywalker, who bolted forward and almost unseated her.

"Serves her right," Holly muttered.

The judge's bell rang and Kate gulped. It was time for her ride. She pulled on her gloves, then gathered up her reins and stared at the arena. The markers blurred and ran together. Her mind went blank.

"I've forgotten the test."

"Duhhhh," Holly said. "You'll remember the minute you get in the ring." She tugged at her cap, the pink one with *Boss Mare* on the front. "And if you don't, Magician will. I bet he could do it without you."

"Good luck," Liz said, slapping Kate's booted leg. "You'll do fine, and don't forget to smile."

Smile?

Kate bared her teeth and hoped it would do. *Come on, brain. Start working.* She trotted a loose circle, then entered the ring. The crowd fell silent. Ahead of her, judge and jury sat beneath an orange-and-white umbrella, pens poised, ready to record comments and scores . . . and mistakes.

* * *

Down the centerline, halt at X. Nod head, smile at judge. This much she could remember. But did she turn right or left at the far end? Magician made the decision for her. He swung to the right and picked up a working trot. Kate's mind cleared, and it all came back. She guided her horse into a circle, then another for a perfect figure eight. At marker H, she slowed to a walk and rounded the short end of the arena. *Don't look at the judge. Head up, eyes ahead. Don't cut corners.*

Concentrate.

On a loose rein, she walked across the diagonal from M to K, then asked for another trot. More circles, left and right. Bigger ones this time, round and full, with Magician curving around her leg like a giant comma. Back to a walk, two strides, and into a canter. Kate sat deep in the saddle and rocked gently, getting that good horse feeling. Magician worked the bit. His ears rotated back, then forward. Back again, waiting for the next signal.

They repeated the same pattern in reverse; and when Kate trotted Magician down the centerline and halted at X, she nodded with confidence at the judge, knowing she'd just done her best. The audience agreed, and she left the ring to enthusiastic applause.

She dropped her reins and wrapped her arms around Magician's neck. He'd barely worked up a sweat. "Good boy," she whispered into his braids. His mane would be curly when she took it out later.

"Nice ride."

Startled, Kate sat up. The boy from Larchwood rubbed Magician's nose, stroked his neck. He was even cuter close up — wavy blond hair, freckles, and green eyes beneath long lashes. He had slender hands with a Scooby Doo Band-Aid wrapped around his little finger.

"Thanks," Kate muttered, suddenly shy.

"Nice horse, too," he said. "What's his name?"

"Magician. He belongs to —"

But then Holly and Liz were there, Robin, too, and Mrs. Shapiro, all talking at once and congratulating her. The boy slipped away.

"Well done," Liz said. "You did a really good job." She took the reins while Kate dismounted, then tossed a fly sheet over Magician's back. "So did you," she added, patting his rump.

"He's a genius," Holly said. "Kate forgot the test, and he did it for her."

"In that case, he deserves the best treatment." Liz handed the reins to Kate. "Walk him out, then put him in his stall and rub him down. Go easy on the water; and when you leave, make sure everything's perfect. There's no reason for us to be faulted on stable management." She turned to Robin. "I want you in bed early tonight. You're riding first thing in the morning." Then she pulled a pad and pencil from her pocket. "I'll go and check on our points so far."

She returned ten minutes later. Predictably, Larchwood was in the lead with a total of 320, Spruce Hill Farm had 312, and Timber Ridge was in third place with 301.

"Mom, that's great," Holly said.

Liz smiled.

"What about the individual points?" Angela asked, still mounted on Skywalker. It didn't look as if she'd cooled him off. The sweat on his shoulders had dried to a white crust.

"They won't be posted till Sunday morning," Liz said, sounding cross. Then her voice softened. "Angela, please try and forget about the medal. We're here as a team, and we need to work together, okay?"

"Whatever," Angela said.

"Now, go and take care of your horse," Liz said. "And don't forget to take out his braids." She turned to the other riders. "That goes for all of you. No braids on the cross-country course."

Angela shrugged. "Come on Denise. Let's get this over with. Mother's waiting." She jerked Skywalker's head, then glanced at Liz. "We'll be at the hotel if you need us."

"Spoiled brat," Holly muttered.

Kate grinned. The rest of them would be crammed

in the Shapiro's motor home for the next two nights. But Kate was looking forward to it. It'd be kind of like a pajama party. She'd never been to one before.

* * *

"Lights out, ladies," Liz said, and not for the first time. "Robin needs her sleep. You'll be zombies in the morning if you —"

"Mom," Holly wailed. "Ten more minutes. Please."

They were playing crazy eights, and she was winning.

Robin yawned and laid down her cards. "Okay, I'm ready," she said. She climbed into the top bunk. Holly and Kate settled into the double bed beneath her.

Liz killed the lights.

"I'm excited about tomorrow," Holly whispered. "Aren't you?"

"No, I'm scared stiff."

"Don't be."

"But what if I mess up?" Kate said.

"My horse won't let you," Holly said. "He's a genius. Remember?"

Kate tried to sleep, but she couldn't stop thinking about the cross-country course. Three-and-a-half miles of trails and jumps through the woods — jumps with scary names like Tiger's Trap, Devil's Drop, and the Witch's Broomstick.

* * *

Kate and Holly reached the start of the cross-country course at nine the next morning. The first rider had just set off. Timers clicked stopwatches, and officials consulted clipboards. Riders circled their horses, anxious to be off.

"I'm going to check the map," Kate said, waving toward a large notice board. Other competitors, including Denise, were gathered in front of it, memorizing the course. She wanted to see where the water hazard lay. Holly had warned her that Magician loved water and that she'd better keep him moving or he'd lie down and roll in it. That had never been a problem with Black Magic. He'd loathed water and would rather jump it than set foot in it. Many a time Kate had almost fallen off as he leaped over a stream the other horses waded through.

For the next few hours, Kate practiced staying calm. Each time she started to worry, she recited nursery rhymes or tried to remember the names of all the horses she'd ever ridden — anything to take her mind off what lay ahead. Robin Shapiro had ridden the course with only five faults. Denise racked up thirty for refusing two fences and for being too slow.

"Remember, it's not a race," Liz warned. "Coming in with a fast time won't get you any extra points. Just keep a steady pace and —"

"Don't let Magician take you for a swim," Holly finished.

Liz gave Kate a leg-up. Like the others, Kate wore the team's cross-country uniform — a green t-shirt beneath her body protector, tan breeches and black boots, and a green-and-white cover on her helmet.

"The worst hazard is all the spectators," Robin warned Kate. "There's a huge crowd at the water and almost as many by the Tiger's Trap. Just watch out for the kids. Chantilly almost took one out. The kid's mother snatched her away just in time."

Angela rode up beside Kate. "I hope you've memorized the course," she said. "I've heard it gets tricky at the end."

"Hurry up, Angela," Liz called out. "They're waiting for you."

"Good luck," Kate said.

Angela stared at her for a moment longer, then turned away.

"She's trying to psyche you out," Holly warned. "Forget her. Pretend you're on the course at home. It's almost the same as this."

But Kate wasn't too sure. Something in Angela's expression told her the girl wasn't through playing tricks.

Not by a long shot.

12

EYES ON THE CLOCK, the timer raised his right arm, then dropped it, and Kate was off. Magician sprang forward like a panther. For the first hundred yards, he fought the bit and wanted to race, but Kate held him back so he'd have enough speed and energy to finish without time faults.

As they approached the first two fences, Kate visualized the course. It reminded her of the puzzles she'd loved as a kid, when you had to find the right path through a maze to reach the treasure. But this one had markers. Red triangles on the right, white on the left. Keep them straight, and you wouldn't get lost.

Magician lengthened his stride and cleared the rustic crossrails, then the brush jump. He bounded up a gentle slope. At the top was a gate made of broom-sticks. The silhouette of a witch's hat hung from the front.

For a second or two, Magician hesitated. His ears flicked back and forth as if to say, *I'm not too sure about this funny looking jump.* Kate agreed. She'd never seen one like this before either. Magician took an extra stride and popped the fence like a pogo stick. His hind legs rapped the top rail, but the gate didn't fall.

That was a close one.

This course was tougher than she expected.

Kate pulled herself together and aimed Magician at the next jump — the dreaded Tiger's Trap. Shortening her reins, she moved into a half-seat, ready for take-off.

Then it happened.

A sudden flash of color — a flag or a piece of cloth — appeared out of nowhere. Magician shied, and Kate lost her balance. She grabbed his mane and righted her-self as Magician swerved the other way. If he circled in front of the jump, they'd be penalized.

"Easy boy," Kate said, using her legs to keep him straight. What had frightened him? She glanced at the crowd and caught sight of Marcia Dean, holding a yellow windbreaker. Was *that* what had scared Magician? Had Angela hired her little sister to do her dirty work for her?

Determination reasserted itself. Kate gritted her teeth and studied the jump. Three rows of logs with enough space between them so the horse could see what was on the other side. A dark, scary ditch! One of Mrs. Mueller's funny sayings shot into her mind.

Throw your heart over the fence, and follow it!

Kate narrowed her eyes and pointed Magician at the jump. One, two, three strides . . . up and over.

Thud! They landed safely on the other side.

People applauded and someone called her name, but Kate's mind was racing ahead. So was Magician. He wanted to run. The footing was dry and firm. Perfect for a gallop.

"Go on, boy," she said. No spectators, no officials. No kids with dangerous clothes. Just her and Holly's beautiful horse. This is what it was all about. Not ribbons and gold medals, but the wind in her face and the power of Magician's muscles as they rippled beneath her. The absolute joy of riding.

The trail forked, and Kate kept to the left, following the red and white markers. Most were on trees, but a few sat on top of black plastic posts like the ones Liz used at the barn when installing electric wire fence. Magician clipped a post as they thundered past, and it fell over. Good thing they were the last to ride the course.

The Devil's Drop came next. Kate felt herself going tense. Two riders had fallen at this combination, and others had refused. She pushed Magician harder. He gathered himself up and flew over the stone wall, cantered down a short bank, then turned a corner and sailed over a chicken coop with colored markers on either side.

"Fabulous," Kate cried.

The trail spilled into a meadow ringed with willows. The water hazard drew closer. Kate slowed to a walk so she could check her watch. They were making excellent time despite their near miss at the Tiger's Trap.

"Okay, boy, no swimming," she warned as they approached the stream and the crowds that had gathered there. Magician's ears pricked. His pace quickened.

"Don't you dare lie down," Kate said.

One of the spectators laughed. "That's telling him."

Magician plunged into the shallow water. He shuddered to a halt and began to paw, first one leg, then the other, splashing like a kid at the beach. Kate's breeches got soaked. Water ran down the inside of her boots. More people laughed, and Kate knew they were hoping she'd take a bath. For the first time ever, she whacked Magician's rump with her crop, glad Holly had insisted she bring it. He lurched forward, and the crowd roared its approval. Kate kept him moving. If he didn't stand still, he wouldn't be able to lie down. When they reached the other side, Magician scrambled up the bank. Kate clung to his mane for fear of slipping off her wet saddle.

"Good boy," she said.

Three more fences to go, but first they had to negotiate the woods. The course map flashed through her mind — winding trails and dead ends. She'd need her wits about her for this part. Too easy to get lost. Kate spotted two markers, both on tree trunks, and rode between them. The trail curved and dipped, then forked. Which way? Standing high in her stirrups, she looked for the next red and white triangles but couldn't see any. There had to be one around here somewhere.

Kate guessed and took the right-hand trail. It narrowed to almost nothing and grew rocky as she pushed her way through the undergrowth. This couldn't be right. Prickers tore at her legs and scratched her hands. Fallen trees barred the way. Kate turned and tried another path, only to find a pile of freshly sawn logs that certainly weren't part of the course.

She visualized the map again. Nothing looked familiar.

"We're lost," she muttered. "I can't find the trail."

Something black lay on the ground. Kate halted and looked closer. An electric fence post, but no sign of its marker. A few yards away, she spotted another post, leaning against a stump. No marker on that one either.

Had Angela done this? Had she destroyed the markers so Kate would get lost? How convenient that they'd drawn the last two numbers. Now what? Stay here till someone came to find them?

Kate wanted to cry with frustration.

Then Magician jerked his head and whirled around. He trotted along yet another trail, and Kate ducked to avoid being swiped by low-hanging branches. He moved faster and faster as if he knew they had to make up for lost time. Finally, the woods gave way to an open field.

Magician flew over the next two fences as if they were no bigger than shoe boxes. Daring to hope they might actually make it, Kate leaned into Magician's sweaty neck as he raced toward the last jump.

13

"WHAT HAPPENED TO YOUR STALL?" Holly cried. "It's a mess."

Kate led Magician inside and gasped. When she'd left to ride the cross-country course, the stall had been clean. She'd picked up the manure, put down fresh shavings, and filled Magician's water bucket. She'd even removed cobwebs from the rafters.

But now, it was a disaster. Droppings littered the ground, and Magician's hay net hung loose from its hook. His fly sheet lay in a heap with a tangle of lead ropes on top. Baling twine, crumpled paper, and dirty leg wraps spilled from an old grain sack.

Angela!

It had to be. Who else would've done this?

"She got me, *again*," Kate muttered, plucking Ma-

* * *

Holly, Robin, and Liz stared at the big time clock on the show secretary's mobile van. Kate had less than two minutes to get back before her time ran out.

"Why is she so late?" Holly asked. Her knuckles turned white as she gripped the wheels of her chair. If only she could stand up. She wanted to see what was going on, but people kept getting in the way.

"Don't worry, she'll make it," her mother said, but she didn't sound convinced. Angela had already finished her ride, but there was still no sign of Kate and Magician.

"She'll get time faults if she doesn't come soon," Holly moaned.

The crowd murmured. Somebody cheered.

"There she is." Liz pushed Holly's chair forward. People parted to let them through. "Oh, Kate, come on. You can make it."

"One more fence," Holly said, holding her breath.

* * *

Kate could feel Magician's energy flagging. He labored up the hill; and as they drew closer to the last obstacle, she remembered with a jolt it was the one she'd been dreading. No way was he going to jump this. Two picnic tables lay end-to-end, covered with a red checkered tablecloth that flapped in the breeze.

Wonderful.

"Don't refuse." Kate rubbed his sweaty neck. "Please, don't refuse."

They cantered closer. Magician's stride faltered, and Kate willed him on with every tired bone in her body. They were so close. She could hear Holly cheering, then Liz's voice telling her she could do it.

"Come on, Kate."

Magician's ears swiveled. Back, then forward. Back again. *Do I really have to?* he seemed to be saying.

Yes.

Why?

Because . . .

As if he'd just sprouted a pair of wings, Magician lifted his great body up and soared over the picnic tables. They landed, and Kate's breath came out in a rush. Another hundred yards, and they swept between the finish posts.

It was over. She'd made it back in one piece. Exhausted and trembling, Kate slid off Magician's back. Sweat covered his shoulders. His mane hung in damp

curls, and his nostrils flared fiery red. Liz threw a blanket over him. She ran her hands down his legs and felt his hooves.

"He's okay," she said. "How about you? What happened out there? Why are you so late getting back?"

"I got lost," Kate said. "Did I get time faults?"

"No," Holly said, grinning. "Ten seconds to spare."

"How about the jumps?" Liz asked. "Any refusals?"

Kate shook her head.

"So you went clear," Liz said, sounding relieved. "Angela did, too, which means we've moved up a notch."

Still half dazed, Kate walked Magician in circles to cool him off. But she was anything *but* cooled off. Her anger at Angela rose and threatened to spill out. Should she confide in Holly? In Liz? Probably not. She had no proof that Angela had destroyed the markers.

Besides, there was only one event left. What could Angela possibly do in the jumping ring in full view of everyone?

* * *

Holly, Robin, and Liz stared at the big time clock on the show secretary's mobile van. Kate had less than two minutes to get back before her time ran out.

"Why is she so late?" Holly asked. Her knuckles turned white as she gripped the wheels of her chair. If only she could stand up. She wanted to see what was going on, but people kept getting in the way.

"Don't worry, she'll make it," her mother said, but she didn't sound convinced. Angela had already finished her ride, but there was still no sign of Kate and Magician.

"She'll get time faults if she doesn't come soon," Holly moaned.

The crowd murmured. Somebody cheered.

"There she is." Liz pushed Holly's chair forward. People parted to let them through. "Oh, Kate, come on. You can make it."

"One more fence," Holly said, holding her breath.

* * *

Kate could feel Magician's energy flagging. He labored up the hill; and as they drew closer to the last obstacle, she remembered with a jolt it was the one she'd been dreading. No way was he going to jump this. Two picnic tables lay end-to-end, covered with a red checkered tablecloth that flapped in the breeze.

Wonderful.

"Don't refuse." Kate rubbed his sweaty neck. "Please, don't refuse."

They cantered closer. Magician's stride faltered, and Kate willed him on with every tired bone in her body. They were so close. She could hear Holly cheering, then Liz's voice telling her she could do it.

"Come on, Kate."

Magician's ears swiveled. Back, then forward. Back again. *Do I really have to?* he seemed to be saying.

Yes.

Why?

Because . . .

As if he'd just sprouted a pair of wings, Magician lifted his great body up and soared over the picnic tables. They landed, and Kate's breath came out in a rush. Another hundred yards, and they swept between the finish posts.

It was over. She'd made it back in one piece. Exhausted and trembling, Kate slid off Magician's back. Sweat covered his shoulders. His mane hung in damp curls, and his nostrils flared fiery red. Liz threw a blanket over him. She ran her hands down his legs and felt his hooves.

"He's okay," she said. "How about you? What happened out there? Why are you so late getting back?"

"I got lost," Kate said. "Did I get time faults?"

"No," Holly said, grinning. "Ten seconds to spare."

"How about the jumps?" Liz asked. "Any refusals?"

Kate shook her head.

"So you went clear," Liz said, sounding relieved. "Angela did, too, which means we've moved up a notch."

Still half dazed, Kate walked Magician in circles to cool him off. But she was anything *but* cooled off. Her anger at Angela rose and threatened to spill out. Should she confide in Holly? In Liz? Probably not. She had no proof that Angela had destroyed the markers.

Besides, there was only one event left. What could Angela possibly do in the jumping ring in full view of everyone?

13

"WHAT HAPPENED TO YOUR STALL?" Holly cried. "It's a mess."

Kate led Magician inside and gasped. When she'd left to ride the cross-country course, the stall had been clean. She'd picked up the manure, put down fresh shavings, and filled Magician's water bucket. She'd even removed cobwebs from the rafters.

But now, it was a disaster. Droppings littered the ground, and Magician's hay net hung loose from its hook. His fly sheet lay in a heap with a tangle of lead ropes on top. Baling twine, crumpled paper, and dirty leg wraps spilled from an old grain sack.

Angela!

It had to be. Who else would've done this?

"She got me, *again*," Kate muttered, plucking Magician's halter off the floor. She wiped off the dirt and buckled it around his neck. Then she adjusted his bucket. Most of the water had spilled, or been tipped, onto the ground.

"What do you mean?" Holly asked.

Kate looked at her. "Sabotage."

There was a pause. "You mean Angela?"

Not trusting herself to speak, Kate pulled off Magician's saddle and bridle, then grabbed a pitchfork and cleaned up as best she could. Holly waited outside, looking in through the metal gate that doubled as a stall door. Beyond her, Kate spotted the couple with clipboards, making notes as they checked stalls along the opposite row. They nodded to one another and walked off. Her stall, obviously, had already been judged.

Kate kicked at a clump of manure. How many points had this cost the team? Five? Ten? Liz had warned everyone the judges were ruthless when it came to sloppy stable management.

"What else has she done?" Holly said.

Kate sighed. No point in holding back. She told Holly about Angela's vandalism on the cross-country course.

"I'm going to tell Mom," Holly sputtered, hands gripping her wheels and ready to roll.

"Don't," Kate said. "She'll only get upset, and she's got enough on her mind as it is." She tossed soiled bedding into a muck bucket. "Besides, there's no point. The competition will be over tomorrow. What else could Angela do?"

"Put a curse on your saddle?"

Kate shrugged. None of this made any sense. If winning was so important to Angela and her mother, why wreck the team's chances? Then again, Angela only cared about the individual gold medal. If the team lost, so what? It'd give Mrs. Dean an excuse to fire Liz, and that would make Angela happy. She'd be only too glad to see the Chapmans, and Kate, leave Timber Ridge.

Holly wheeled herself out of sight. Then she called out, "Hey, you'd better come and see this."

"What's wrong?"

"That," Holly said. She peered through the bars of the stall across from theirs. Inside stood the flashy black-and-white gelding that belonged to the boy from Larchwood. One of its leg wraps had come loose.

Kate unlatched the gate.

"What are you going to do?" Holly said.

"Fix it," Kate replied.

"Why?"

"Because if I don't, he'll step on it and panic."

"But he's a rival," Holly said. "He'll lose points for this." She waved toward the horse. "Besides, you can't just go in there and —"

Kate pushed Holly's chair to one side and slipped into the stall. The pinto snorted and backed away, nostrils extended and eyes showing white.

"Easy, boy," Kate said, holding out her hand. He sniffed it, then tossed his head and snorted again.

"Better tie him up," Holly said from the doorway.

Moving slowly, Kate clipped a lead rope to the pinto's halter and secured him to a ring on the wall. He shivered and pinned his ears; Kate stroked his neck, speaking softly as she ran a hand down his shoulder. So far, so good. She was about to undo the leg wrap, when someone came up behind her.

"What do you think you're doing?"

Kate whirled around. She took in the blond hair, green eyes, and little finger with a cartoon Band-Aid. "I'm just —"

He scowled and reached for his horse's halter.

"I was only trying to help," Kate said, blushing.

The pinto yanked on its rope. The boy unclipped it. "He hates being tied up."

"I'm sorry," Kate mumbled. "I didn't know." She backed out of the stall. Holly was right. She should've left well enough alone. The boy probably thought she was trying to mess things up — like Angela had.

Holly's face was alive with questions. "What did he say?"

Kate told her.

"He's a jerk," Holly said, loud enough for him to hear. "You were only doing him a favor, *and* rescuing his stupid horse." She pointed toward the food booth. "Let's get a hot dog."

They bought french fries and jumbo franks loaded with onions, mustard, and relish. Kate was about to bite into hers when the boy from Larchwood approached their table.

"Hey, I'm sorry," he said, looking at her. "I shouldn't have blown up. You were only trying to help." He paused and shuffled his feet. "Can I sit down?"

"Yeah, I guess."

"I'm Adam Randolph," he said. "Super-jerk." He rolled his eyes and stuck his thumbs in his ears.

Kate burst out laughing. "I'm Kate McGregor," she said. "And that's Holly Chapman. We're from Timber Ridge."

"I know," Adam said. "My mother told me about you."

Holly slapped her forehead. "Randolph," she said, dragging out the syllables. "Then your mom's one of the —"

"— therapeutic riding volunteers," Adam finished. "My sister has muscular dystrophy. Mom's been teaching her to ride."

"She's great," Holly said. "She really helped me . . . a lot."

Eyeing their food, Adam said, "Looks good. I'm starving." Then he shot Kate a sheepish grin. "I'm sorry for yelling at you. It's just that Domino can be difficult with strangers," he said, sneaking a french fry. "I thought you were trying to —"

"Sabotage you?" Holly said.

He blushed. "Yes."

Holly snorted. "There's only one person around here who does that," she said. "And it isn't Kate McGregor. It's —"

"*Holly!*" Kate warned, as Angela and Denise wandered up. Their freshly washed hair and clean clothes made Kate feel like a grub. She ran a hand across her sweaty forehead.

"Adam," Angela said, ignoring Kate and Holly. "My parents are having a barbecue at the hotel. Want to come and join us?"

He glanced at Kate, then looked up at Angela. "Thanks, but I already ate."

Holly choked and spat crumbs in her lap.

"Pity," Denise said. "We've got steak and corn-on-the-cob." She sniffed and glanced at Holly's face, streaked with mustard and ketchup. "Better company, too."

Adam shrugged. "Sorry," he said. "Maybe next time."

He didn't sound as if he meant it, and Kate had to bite her lip to keep from laughing out loud at Angela's sour expression. Holly's face was turning pink, and she looked ready to explode into giggles. Funny thing was, Adam didn't seem to realize how pissed off Angela was. Or did he? Was he trying to hold back a smile? He took another fry and winked at Kate.

* * *

That night after the others had gone to sleep, Holly teased Kate about Adam. Kate told her to shut up but then found herself thinking it was kind of nice to meet a boy who loved horses as much as she did. Adam had hung out with them till dark, cracking jokes and making them laugh with his imitation of the Larch-wood riding coach, who wore old-fashioned riding breeches and whose favorite saying seemed to be "If at first you don't succeed, do it again without stirrups."

Adam's coach sounded just like Mrs. Mueller.

* * *

Early the next morning, Liz handed out orange juice and doughnuts. Her riders stood outside the Shapiro's van, stamping their feet, trying to keep warm. Once the mist cleared up, it'd be plenty hot; but right now Kate wished she'd packed an extra sweater. Wrapped in Holly's down vest, she'd already been to the stables and fed Magician. Then she'd taken pity on Skywalker and Luna and fed them as well because, as usual, Angela and Denise had failed to show up on time.

There was still no word about individual points, so Kate had no idea where she stood. The team was now in second place, twenty-two points behind Larchwood Equestrian Club and one point ahead of Spruce Hill Farm. Kate hadn't told Liz about Magician's messy stall; if it hadn't been for Angela, the team might've been in the lead. Who knows how many points they'd lost for sloppy stable management. Kate was worried Liz would chide her for being lax, but nothing was said. Holly told her it was because the judges didn't say *why* someone was penalized. The teams wouldn't know the reasons for their penalties until after the competition was over.

Liz was optimistic. "You guys are doing your best, and that's all I care about right now."

Kate wondered if perhaps she and Holly worried more about Liz's job than Liz did herself. Except for the occasional raised eyebrow and furrowed brow whenever Mrs. Dean interfered, Liz seemed to have it all under control.

Liz drank the last of her coffee. "Okay, Robin. Let's get moving." She grabbed her windbreaker and ushered her first rider toward the stables. An hour later, Robin completed the jumping course with only ten faults, but Denise's horse refused three times, and they were eliminated from the competition. Luna left the ring with her nose in the air, ears back and fighting the bit.

"I'm not surprised," Holly muttered.

No other riders had been dropped, which meant

Timber Ridge was the only team with three members. How would this affect their score? Kate asked Liz.

"Do we still have a chance?"

"Of course," Liz said, checking her notes. "Larchwood has one more rider to jump, and right now they've got 275 points. We have 266, and Spruce Hill is all through with 225."

Kate did a rapid calculation. "So, if Angela and I have clear rounds and Larchwood's last rider gets more than nine faults, we'll win?"

Liz grinned. "Something like that, yes." She gave Kate a leg-up. "Now, go and warm up your horse, and stop worrying, okay?"

After walking and trotting in circles, Kate rode Magician over the practice fences, then halted long enough to watch the last Larchwood rider jump the course. Not Adam. He'd already gone clear, and Kate and Holly had cheered him on, despite dirty looks from Angela and Denise. The bay gelding now in the ring was doing well, and so far he hadn't refused or knocked anything down. Kate held her breath as he approached the last two jumps, then let out a sigh of relief as his hind legs rapped the top bar hard enough to make it fall. Off balance, the horse stumbled and ran out at the last fence. His rider brought him back and tried again. He leaped over it, but the damage was done. They'd racked up ten faults.

Timber Ridge had a fighting chance.

It was up to her and Angela now.

14

Once again, Angela pushed all the right buttons. Skywalker cleared one fence after another, and the crowd cheered as they left the ring with a clean round. Angela swept past Kate and shot her a look that said, *Beat that if you can*.

"Well done," Liz called out.

Angela swept past her as well, then skidded Skywalker to a halt like a cutting horse. Sides heaving, he whirled around, and something bright flashed at Angela's heels.

Kate looked closer.

Spurs?

No wonder they'd jumped the course in record time. Not that it counted. They weren't riding against the clock. Angela peeled off her gloves and unbuttoned her jacket. Denise rushed up.

"You're going to win the medal," she squealed.

"No way," Holly growled.

Liz put her hand on Kate's thigh. "Are you ready?"

Kate swallowed hard and nodded. She was as ready as could be. Behind her, Mrs. Dean showered Angela with questions. Was she in the lead? How many points did she have? Would she have to ride again?

Kate felt an unexpected pang of pity for Angela. No wonder she was such a brat. Then her heart skipped a beat as she heard her own mother's voice the day of her first show. She was seven and riding Webster, the barn's beginner pony. They hadn't won a ribbon. Hadn't even come close, but her mother had hugged them both and said it didn't matter, that knowing you'd tried your best and feeling good about yourself was more important than winning ribbons. Pity Mrs. Dean hadn't taught Angela the same lesson.

Liz's voice broke in. "Kate, are you listening?"

Her stomach tightened. "Yes."

"Don't let Magician rush his fences," Liz said. "He'll try to race, but you have to stop him. Keep him collected on that turn before the parallel bars. And watch out for the double oxer. It's quite a spread."

Kate gulped. At this point she didn't want any more directions, any more responsibility. She'd like for this to be all over. She glanced at Liz's anxious face. Three weeks ago, she'd never heard of Timber Ridge or Liz and Holly Chapman. Yet now, for the next few minutes, it seemed as if their future was in her hands. Robin slapped Magician's rump and wished them good luck. Then Kate caught sight of Adam in the bleachers. He gave her a thumbs up. Good thing his teammates weren't there. They'd have killed him. Two rows over, Aunt Marion sat between Mrs. Shapiro and Sue Piretti. It was Sue's first day out since the accident. They all waved at Kate. With this much support, how could she possibly fail?

Easy . . . all she had to do was fall off, or misjudge a fence, or —

The announcer called Kate's number.

Holly tugged at her stirrup. "I've crossed my fingers, and if I could move my toes, I'd cross those as well." Leaning forward, she grabbed one foot and lifted it over the other. "Like this." Then she sat up and said, "Oh."

"What's wrong?" her mother said.

"I think I felt something."

"Where?"

"My foot," Holly said. "It tingles."

Liz crouched and ran her hands along Holly's thighs, down her calves, massaging her muscles. "Feel anything?"

"Nope."

"How about this?" Liz rotated Holly's feet.

Holly sighed and slumped back in her chair. "Nothing."

"Are you sure?"

"False alarm," Holly said. "I'm imagining things."

Kate let out her breath, unaware she'd been holding it. Poor Holly. Another disappointment. She was about to jump off Magician and give her friend a hug, when the ring steward bustled up and told Liz to get her last rider in the ring.

"Hurry up," Holly said. "Or you'll be disqualified."

Kate checked her girth. Then Liz took Magician's reins and led him toward the gate, as if she didn't trust Kate to get him there herself. The sun chose that moment to show itself. Until now, the day had been bright but overcast — perfect for jumping. No light reflecting off car windshields or blinding a horse and rider as they approached a fence. And now, at four o'clock, the sun was lower in the sky, which made it even worse. Just her rotten luck. Kate blinked and tugged her helmet down. If only she'd worn sunglasses.

Too late for that now.

Liz let go of the reins. "Good luck."

"Thanks." Kate trotted into the ring. Eight jumps lay between her and the team's victory. Could she pull it off without mishap?

The starter's whistle blew.

Magician catapulted forward. He cleared the cross-rail and raced toward the brush jump. Up and over he went, feet grazing the twigs but not doing any damage except for scattering a few more leaves on the ground. They turned the corner, and Kate remembered Liz's instructions. She asked Magician to come back to her and he responded.

"Easy, fella," she whispered, and his ears swiveled like antenna, waiting for her next signal. Sitting deep in her saddle, Kate counted his strides.

"One, two" — she leaned forward — "three, and up."

With a massive push, he launched himself at the parallel bars.

They were flying and it was great . . .

And then it wasn't.

Kate lurched to one side. Her right leg gave way and it felt as if she'd just stepped in a hole.

What . . . ?

Her stirrup flew off and clanged against the jump. Kate grabbed Magician's mane, the front of her saddle . . . anything to keep from falling off.

"Aarrgghhh!" groaned the crowd.

Pulse racing, Kate struggled for balance. She hauled herself upright and kicked her other foot free of its stirrup. Reaching for the leather, she slung it across the pommel. Far safer to ride with no stirrups than just one.

"Atta girl!" a man shouted. "You can do it!"

Yeah, right.

Kate angled Magician toward the double oxer. "Don't jump too big," she warned, as he approached the red-and-white poles. His stride grew bolder, and he arced over the fence with Kate almost hugging his neck and praying that somehow she'd stay on his back

The audience clapped, but Kate barely heard them. Already, her legs ached, and she longed for the relief that stirrups would bring. Cutting diagonally across the ring, she faced her horse at the gate. One-and-a-half strides behind it lay the barrels. A tricky combination. Could she manage it without stirrups?

Half-blinded by the sun, Kate felt Magician shoot off the ground. His neck rose toward her. She thrust her arms forward, then her shoulders. Her body followed, and her cheek grazed his mane, still curly despite her best efforts with a wet brush that morning. They landed far beyond the gate. One huge stride, then up and over the barrels, and Kate felt as if she were floating because most of her wasn't in the saddle. It was up in the air.

Would they ever land?

Clods of dirt flew up as Magician's forelegs hit the ground.

Two more jumps.

The audience fell quiet, and all Kate could hear was Magician's heavy breathing and the thump, thump, thump of his hooves as they approached the next-to-last fence — a black-and-white striped railroad crossing with fake lanterns and red stop signs on either side. It was so realistic that Kate wouldn't have been surprised to see a train chugging up the tracks.

Magician snorted, then cleared it with ease.

"Good boy," she said, rubbing his sweat-covered neck. Another ten seconds and all this would be over. She could let go and just fall off.

They turned the last corner, into the sun again. Kate

blinked, then squinted at the wall — red and solid with poles on top and white wings to the side and flower boxes in front. Several horses had stopped dead at this jump, probably because it looked good enough to eat, Holly had said.

Magician raced toward it. Kate's legs screamed for mercy. Good thing this was all about jumping fences and not about style. Hers had gone down the tubes with her stirrup. Magician picked up speed. Kate tried to hold him back, but it was too late. The sun blinded her, and she couldn't see the jump any more. How many more strides? Two? Three? Magician tucked in an extra one and took off too close.

They were going to knock it down . . . or crash into it.

Magician leaped straight up in the air, and Kate had a mental picture of the poster in Holly's room, the one with the Lipizzaner doing a levade, its rider without stirrups.

Just like her.

Magician's neck collided with Kate's nose. She closed her eyes.

We're not gonna make it!

The crowd sucked in its collective breath. Kate felt herself losing contact. She slid backward. This was it.

This was where she was going to fall off. In desperation, she grasped Magician's mane and held on. He twisted his body and bunched his legs beneath his belly, and somehow they landed on the other side and kept going.

Kate was flabbergasted to find herself still in the saddle.

Scenery and spectators rushed by like speeded-up film.

Flashes of color, snatches of noise. Cheering. People yelling her name.

It took a few seconds for it all to sink in.

They were cheering for her, for the team.

Had they won the Classic?

Trembling with exhaustion, Kate steered Magician out of the ring. Liz helped her dismount; and when Kate's feet hit the ground, she crumpled into a heap. Her fingers held strands of Magician's mane, and her shoulders ached with tension. She couldn't even feel her legs.

"Did I go clear?" she mumbled, head down.

"And how!" Liz said. "Can't you hear them? The crowd is still cheering."

"We won!" Holly shrieked. "We won the challenge cup."

"Don't celebrate yet," her mother said. "It's too close to call." She ran a hand through her hair. "I could've miscalculated our points."

Kate tried to stand, but her legs were too weak. She sat down again, hard.

"Kate!" Liz said. "Your nose. It's bleeding." She pulled a wad of tissues from her pocket.

"Thanks." Kate put a hand to her face and felt a warm, sticky wetness. "Magician whacked me," she said, sniffing. The blood dribbled over her lips and tasted gross. "At the last jump," she added, still in shock they'd gotten over it. She was so sure they were going to crash.

Magician lowered his head and nudged Kate. In a daze, she circled his nose with one arm, still pressing her own nose to stem the bleeding. The tissues were soaked. Liz gave her more.

One of the stewards ran up with Kate's flyaway stirrup.

Liz thanked him, then squatted beside Kate. "What happened out there?" she said. "Why did it come off?"

Kate shrugged. "Guess it wasn't on properly."

"Did you check?"

"No, but I tightened my girth before I went in the

ring," Kate said. "Same side as the stirrup. I probably loosened it."

"Well, thank goodness you weren't hurt," Liz said, helping Kate to her feet. "You put on an amazing display, jumping without stirrups."

"Will they give her bonus points?" Holly asked.

"Dream on," Liz replied. She tossed a blanket over Magician and handed his reins to Robin. "Walk him around for a bit, okay?" Then Mrs. Dean claimed her attention with more questions about the individual medal and why Liz didn't ask the judge if they'd won the team trophy. Surely they knew the results by now.

* * *

Holly pointed at the stirrup, still in Kate's hand. "They don't go flying into outer space without help."

"It was an accident."

"I *warned* you," Holly said. "She put a curse on your saddle."

"Holly, don't even go there," Kate said. "The competition's over. There's nothing else Angela can do to wreck it."

"Hah!" Holly said. "That's what you think."

Kate dabbed her nose. Had Angela really interfered

with that stirrup? Easy enough to do — just slide the leather to the end of the bar and, pretty soon, it'd come loose. She could've been injured. *Killed.* Was Angela *that* desperate to win?

Despite the sweat trickling down her neck, Kate shivered. She didn't want to believe Angela could've done something so monumentally dumb . . . and dangerous. It was one thing to move course markers and mess up a stall, but tampering with a stirrup? Well, Kate had no answer for that.

Angela interrupted her thoughts. "Did I win the medal?"

"Oh, shut up!" Holly snapped. "Can't you think about anything else?"

The loudspeaker drowned Angela's reply.

"Ladies and gentlemen. Before we announce the team winners, we'd like to bring you up to date on the individual medal." There was a pause. "We have two riders tied for first place."

15

A HUSH FELL OVER THE CROWD. Conversations died as people turned toward the loudspeaker. In the collecting ring, two riding coaches halted mid-gossip. Even Angela and Denise stopped whispering long enough to listen. Kate caught her breath. What if *she* were one of the lucky riders?

The announcer continued. "Will numbers thirty-one and thirty-two please come to the judge's stand?"

Leaving Denise to hold her horse, Angela strode toward the ring. At the gate, she stopped and turned, looking directly at Kate, her face a mask of contempt. It was so full of loathing that Kate wanted to shrink inside her jacket . . . to be so small nobody could see her.

"Go on, you dummy," Holly said, shoving Kate forward.

Kate almost fell over. "What did you do that for?"

"Well, duhh-uh," Holly said. "Are you number thirty-two, or what?"

Kate gulped. She ripped the cardboard numbers off her arm and stared at them. A three and a two stared back.

"Hurry up," Holly said. "They'll think you don't want it."

"I'll go with you," Liz said, grabbing Kate's hand. Angela was already in the ring, standing in front of the judge. His bowler hat leaned at a rakish angle over his face. Red suspenders peeked from beneath his yellow vest.

"Congratulations, ladies," he said. "Are you their instructor, ma'am?" He nodded toward Liz.

She smiled. "Yes."

The judge held up a gold medal. "We have a problem," he said. "We weren't expecting a tie, and we only have one of these So if you have no objections, I'd like your two riders to share it." He offered the medal to Liz.

She looked at Kate, raised an eyebrow. "Well?"

Kate swallowed hard. Was the judge nuts? This was like asking two horses to share the same carrot. No way would this work. But for Liz's sake, she had to try. She put a hand on Angela's shoulder. "We've *both* won. Let's split the prize."

Angela brushed Kate's hand away, then scowled at the judge. "Can't we have a ride-off instead?" she asked.

He coughed and checked his watch. "I suppose we could."

"Angela," Liz protested. "The horses are wiped out."

Me, too, Kate thought. Her legs trembled. Her arms ached. Even her toenails were tired.

"Skywalker's fine," Angela snapped. Arms folded, she challenged the judge. "So, what do we have to do?"

"That's enough, Angela," Liz said.

The judge consulted his assistant. They shuffled papers back and forth, and the judge nodded several times. "We'll make another announcement shortly," he said.

Kate's heart sank. She didn't want to ride again. Her legs couldn't stand the punishment. "Come on, Angela," she said. "Let's toss for it."

"No, we'll ride!" Angela turned and stalked off.

Liz put her arm around Kate's shoulders. "Thanks for trying to patch things up," she said. "I know she's not easy to work with, and I appreciate your effort."

Biting back her frustration, Kate followed Liz from the ring. Holly waited by the gate. "What's going to happen?" she asked.

Kate told her.

"You'll win," Holly said, grinning. "Easy, peasy."

The loudspeaker crackled into life. "Will both finalists lead their horses into the ring."

Kate stripped off Magician's blanket and draped it over the back of Holly's chair. Angela marched past, leading a reluctant Skywalker. He dragged his feet and lacked his usual pep and energy. Maybe he'd had enough, too. Kate knew she had. But Magician, obviously, didn't agree. He pushed Kate with his nose. She may have been exhausted, but he seemed willing to give it another try.

She trailed after her teammate, back into the ring.

* * *

Angela's eyes widened with horror when the judge explained what he wanted them to do.

"Switch horses?" she cried. "That's not fair."

He pinned her with a look. "You could always toss for it."

Kate saw Angela's hesitation and had no trouble figuring out what was running through her mind.

Her mother — the driving force behind Angela's need to win.

Kate glanced toward Holly and Liz, waiting anxiously with Robin and Denise. Beside them, Mrs. Dean and her outrageous straw hat made a gaudy splash of color against the muted tones of riding clothes and horses. From the expression on her face, it was obvious she expected her daughter to win. No way could Angela back down now. Mrs. Dean would never forgive her if she gambled on the flip of a coin.

"I'll ride," Angela said. She tucked her whip beneath one arm and pulled on her gloves. Then she reached for Magician's reins. "And I'll ride first."

They switched horses. "Go easy on his mouth," Kate said.

"Don't tell me how to ride," Angela snapped. Sticking her foot in the stirrup, she swung her leg over Magician's back and landed in the saddle like a sack of potatoes. Sunlight glinted off her spurs.

"You won't need those," Kate said. "Take them off."

Angela dug in her heels and Magician leaped forward.

It'd serve her right, Kate thought, *if he bucked her off.*

Kate's apprehension grew as Angela tried to control Magician. He stuck his nose in the air and evaded the bit. Angela used her legs and her voice, but he refused to pick up the right lead. He wasn't a push-button horse. Kate considered her options. If she rode Skywalker, she'd beat Angela for the medal. No question. And, oh, how she wanted to beat her, fair and square in front of an audience . . . *and* Angela's miserable mother.

Then reality kicked in. Kate's heart missed a beat.

What was she thinking?

This would be a disaster. Thoughts of Liz's job and Mrs. Dean's power over the homeowners' committee shot through her mind. She pictured Liz and Holly packing up their house, finding another place to live, another job for Liz. She glanced at Angela again. The girl was about to use her crop.

That did it.

Kate led Skywalker over to the judge. "I've changed my mind," she said. "I'm withdrawing."

He looked at her in astonishment. "Why?"

"My leg hurts," she said, using the first excuse that leaped into her head. "I can't ride."

The judge looked at her for a moment as if he didn't quite believe her, then he nodded. Kate turned away, determined not to let him see her tears. She limped back to the gate and handed Skywalker's reins to Denise as the announcer informed an astonished audience that the winner of the individual gold medal was Angela Dean from Timber Ridge.

After a round of polite applause, the judge placed the medal around Angela's neck and pinned the red, white, and blue ribbon to Magician's bridle. Holly's horse made a victory pass around the ring accompanied by scattered cheers. Kate glanced at the bleachers, hoping to spot Adam. He was no longer there.

"That should've been *your* ribbon," Holly said.

Kate shrugged. "At least it's on the right horse."

"But —"

Horses and riders pushed past them. More followed, and Liz grabbed Holly's chair and pulled it out of the way as competitors milled about, waiting to hear the final results. Moments later, Angela rode up and jumped off Magician's back. She snatched the ribbon from his bridle, then thrust the reins at Kate.

"Here's your stupid horse," she snapped, eyes flashing with triumph. "I beat you, Kate McGregor. Fair and square. You chickened out!"

"No, I did *not*," Kate said, keeping her voice low so nobody else would hear. "If you hadn't fouled things up, I'd have beaten you."

Angela's face paled.

"You trashed the course markers so I'd get lost," Kate said, "then you wrecked Magician's stall."

"I did not," Angela snapped.

"And on top of that," Kate said, beginning to enjoy herself, "you messed with my stirrups." She glared at Angela. "I could've been killed."

Angela stepped back, and Kate knew she'd hit the mark.

"Don't blame me because you can't ride," Angela said. "It's your fault you lost. You weren't good enough to win."

"I'll win next time," Kate said. "And you can't stop me."

"Ha! There won't be a *next* time," Angela said. "You'll never ride for the team again. My mother will see to that."

Still wearing her ridiculous shoes, Mrs. Dean rushed up.

"Well done, darling." She pecked Angela on the cheek. Kate almost choked. She'd never seen Mrs. Dean show affection before, not even for the yappy little terrier that rode in the front seat of her car and slobbered all over the windows.

"I knew you'd win," her mother went on, leading Angela toward a group of women wearing silk dresses and high heels. Definitely not horse people. "We'll display your new medal with all the others," Mrs. Dean said. "And I can't wait to show . . ."

Angela turned and looked back. Her eyes connected with Kate's and for a split second Kate felt as if they were nothing more complicated than two teenage girls who loved horses and hoped to have a boyfriend one day. Then Angela blinked. Her face settled into its customary sneer, and the moment was gone. Kate sighed. Giving up that medal had hurt, but not as much as Magician would've been hurt if Angela had used her whip and spurs to get him over those jumps.

Holly's voice slid into her thoughts as if on rollerblades. "Why did you let her win?"

"Didn't you see the way she mauled Magician?"

"Yes, but —"

Kate nodded toward Liz, chatting with Mrs. Dean and her overdressed friends. Their voices gushed with admiration and lavish praise. Maybe now that the medal was safely in Angela's hands, Liz could stop worrying about getting fired. At least, for another year.

Holly exhaled. "Thanks for saving my horse," she finally said. "*And* my mother's job."

"What's that about my job?" Liz asked.

Holly jumped. So did Kate. She hadn't heard Liz walk up.

"You tell her," Holly said, nudging Kate.

Kate dug at a clump of grass with her toe. Taking a deep breath, she said, "Holly figured you'd lose your job if the team didn't win blue ribbons, and —"

"— Kate let Angela win so Mrs. Dean wouldn't be mad at you," Holly finished.

Liz stared at Kate. "You threw in the towel because of that?"

"Mom, you know what Mrs. Dean's like. She —"

"Mrs. Dean doesn't dictate to me," Liz said, shaking her head. "Where'd you get that crazy idea?"

"From you?" Holly said, so quietly Kate barely heard her.

Liz knelt in front of Holly's chair and reached for her daughter's hands. "If I gave you that impression, I'm sorry. Really sorry. I didn't mean to." She looked up at Kate, eyes full of concern. "I had no idea Holly convinced you I was in jeopardy."

"But, Mom, we thought —"

"Holly, calm down," her mother said. "I love you for worrying about my job, but that's my responsibility. Not yours. No matter what Angela says, I'm not in danger of losing it." She smiled. "In fact, Mrs. Shapiro just told me the committee wants to extend my contract for another three years."

"Oh, Mom, that's great," Holly cried.

Turning away, Kate stifled a sob. That medal could've been hers. She really wanted to beat Angela, to make her pay for all the awful things she'd said and done.

"Kate, I'm sorry," Liz said. "You deserved that medal. I wish there was some way I could —"

A rush of static erupted from the loudspeaker. "Ladies and gentlemen," it boomed. "You'll be glad to know we have the results."

The crowd went quiet again.

"The winner of this year's Hampshire County Classic is the team from Timber Ridge Stables, and in second place . . ."

Holly and Robin shrieked, Liz wiped a stray tear,

and Kate felt a warm glow inside. They'd done it. Despite Angela's sabotage, the team had won. Kate wrapped her arms around Magician's neck. "Thanks," she whispered into his soft, silky mane. "You're the best horse in the world."

"Yeah, he is, but don't tell Domino."

She looked up and saw Adam grinning down at her. Larchwood had taken second place.

"I'll catch you later," he said and rode off.

Holly let rip with an ear-splitting whoop. Kate blushed and wanted to die. Liz gave her a leg-up, and she landed in the saddle, grateful for even this small diversion. She stuck her feet in the stirrups and followed her teammates into the ring. Behind her came Liz, pushing Holly. The crowd cheered. Aunt Marion, Mrs. Shapiro, and Sue Piretti waved and blew kisses from the bleachers.

The judge held up the trophy. Angela rode forward.

"Not this time," Liz said. She took hold of Skywalker's reins.

Angela tried to snatch them away, but Liz held firm. She nodded at Kate. "Go on," she said. "This one's for you."

Kate hesitated. "Are you sure?"

"Hurry up," Holly said.

Magician tossed his head and pranced sideways. Then he settled down and allowed the judge to pin a gold-and-blue ribbon to his bridle.

"Congratulations," the judge said, handing Kate the challenge trophy. "That was a spectacular ride. I don't know how you pulled it off, but I'm glad you did." He tipped his hat and pinned first-place ribbons on the other three Timber Ridge horses.

Loving the way it felt, Kate hugged the silver statue of horse and rider to her face. Its smooth metal cooled her flushed cheeks and reminded her of the heavy jewelry her mother used to wear.

Trying your best and feeling good about yourself is more important than winning prizes.

Kate didn't care about the gold medal any more. That was Angela's prize. This trophy belonged to the team, to Liz and Holly and the riders at Timber Ridge. They'd earned it the hard way.

"Let me see it," Holly said.

Kate bent to give her the trophy. It slipped from her hands and landed on Holly's foot.

"Ouch," Holly cried. "That hurt."

There was a stunned silence.

"What did you say?" Kate asked.

Holly burst into tears. "It hurts."

"Good grief," Liz said. She dropped to her knees and cradled Holly's foot. "You know what this means, don't you?"

"Yes," Holly said, laughing through her tears. She looked at her mother, then at Kate. "It means I'm going to walk, and then I'm going to ride Magician, and this time next year —"

"— you'll beat me?" Kate said.

Holly grinned. "You got it."

Kate grinned back. She had a strong feeling that, for once, Holly was dead serious.

Don't miss **Book 2** in the exciting
Timber Ridge Riders series.

Racing into Trouble

Ever since Kate McGregor arrived at Timber
Ridge Stables, Angela Dean has been
making trouble for her. Maybe she's angry
because Kate's a better rider than she is, or
maybe she's jealous because Kate's the only
one who's allowed to ride Buccaneer, the
barn's willful new horse. To further
complicate matters, a new girl — Jennifer
West — moves into the neighborhood and
Angela sets out to impress her.

But when Angela makes a fool of herself
in front of Jennifer, things begin to go wrong
and Kate gets the blame. Is Angela behind
the trouble? Kate and her best friend, Holly
Chapman who's learning to walk and ride
again, can't be sure.

But they do know one thing. If Angela's
on the warpath, Kate is heading for trouble,
and fast.

Sign up for our mailing list and be among the first to know when the next Timber Ridge Riders book will be out. Send your email address to:

timberridgeriders@gmail.com

For more information about the series, visit:
www.timberridgeriders.com

or check out our Facebook page:
www.facebook.com/TimberRidgeRiders

Note: all email addresses are kept strictly confidential.

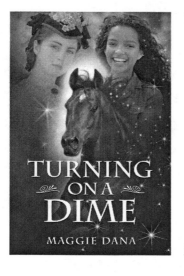

Two girls, two centuries apart, and the horse that brings them together

TURNING ON A DIME

This exciting time-travel adventure (with horses, of course) from the author of TIMBER RIDGE RIDERS is available in print and ebook from your favorite book store.

For information and to read an excerpt, visit:
www.maggiedana.com

About the Author

Maggie Dana's first riding lesson, at the age of five, was less than wonderful. She hated it so much, she didn't try again for another three years. But all it took was the right horse and the right instructor and she was hooked.

After that, Maggie begged for her own pony and was lucky enough to get one. Smoky was a black New Forest pony who loved to eat vanilla pudding and drink tea, and he became her constant companion. Maggie even rode him to school one day and tethered him to the bicycle rack ... but not for long because all the other kids wanted pony rides, much to their teachers' dismay.

Maggie and Smoky competed in Pony Club trials and won several ribbons. But mostly, they had fun — trail riding and hanging out with other horse-crazy girls. At horse camp, Maggie and her teammates spent one night sleeping in the barn, except they didn't get much sleep because the horses snored. The next morning, everyone was tired and cranky, especially when told to jump without stirrups.

Born and raised in England, Maggie now makes her home on the Connecticut shoreline. When not mucking stalls or grooming shaggy ponies, Maggie enjoys spending time with her family and writing the next book in her TIMBER RIDGE RIDERS series.

CPSIA information can be obtained at www.ICGtesting.com
Printed in the USA
LVOW11s1759180416

484151LV00007B/733/P